P9-DEV-584

A Fairytale Summer!

Can the magic of friendship lead to love?

Once upon a time...

Jessica, Daisy and Aubrey left a Copenhagen music festival as lifelong friends after coming to the rescue of an adorable dog and his eternally grateful owner. What they didn't realize is that they'd also left the festival with...

...a fairy godmother

CEO Vivian Ascot has watched over the three women ever since their extraordinary act of kindness. And it saddens her to see how they've gradually lost sight of their dreams over the years. So, this summer she anonymously bequeaths each of the girls a special gift to nudge them toward...

...happy-ever-after

They just need to find the courage to believe that each of Viv's gifts could bring them a lifetime of happiness—and to embrace fun and romance along the way!

Discover Jessica's story in
Cinderella's New York Fling by Cara Colter

Read Daisy's story in
Italian Escape with Her Fake Fiancé
by Sophie Pembroke

And find Aubrey's story in
Dream Vacation, Surprise Baby by Ally Blake

All available now!

Dear Reader,

My books always begin with the tiniest idea. A funny opening line. Some small situation that tickles my fancy. This one was no different.

The original concept of this story was no more than an image of a young Australian woman standing before the statue of the *David* in Florence when a man steps up beside her, says something, and she realizes he's Australian, too. That's it! A single moment. One I jotted down ten years ago.

The idea finally found its purpose when I was asked to contribute to a trilogy alongside wonderful writers Cara Colter and Sophie Pembroke. A Canadian, a Brit and an Aussie author—it had to be an international travel fest, right? And hadn't I once had an idea about a girl in Florence? I think ideas find their own moment. My young Australian woman, Aubrey, would not be the same joyful, indomitable character she is without the time spent brewing in Cara's and Sophie's delightful stories first.

So snuggle in and let me whisk you away to Florence! And if you don't also have a crush on the *David* by the end, well, then there's more of him for me. ;)

Love,

Ally

Dream Vacation, Surprise Baby

Ally Blake

If you purchased this book without a cover you should be aware that this book is stolen property. It was reported as "unsold and destroyed" to the publisher, and neither the author nor the publisher has received any payment for this "stripped book."

Recycling programs
for this product may
not exist in your area.

ISBN-13: 978-1-335-55642-4

Dream Vacation, Surprise Baby

Copyright © 2020 by Ally Blake

All rights reserved. No part of this book may be used or reproduced in any manner whatsoever without written permission except in the case of brief quotations embodied in critical articles and reviews.

This is a work of fiction. Names, characters, places and incidents are either the product of the author's imagination or are used fictitiously. Any resemblance to actual persons, living or dead, businesses, companies, events or locales is entirely coincidental.

This edition published by arrangement with Harlequin Books S.A.

For questions and comments about the quality of this book, please contact us at CustomerService@Harlequin.com.

Harlequin Enterprises ULC
22 Adelaide St. West, 40th Floor
Toronto, Ontario M5H 4E3, Canada
www.Harlequin.com

Printed in U.S.A.

Australian author **Ally Blake** loves reading and strong coffee, porch swings and dappled sunshine, beautiful notebooks and soft, dark pencils. Her inquisitive, rambunctious, spectacular children are her exquisite delights. And she adores writing love stories so much she'd write them even if nobody else read them. No wonder, then, having sold over four million copies of her romance novels worldwide, Ally is living her bliss. Find out more about Ally's books at allyblake.com.

Dedicated to Em. For the bit about the horse.

Oh, and the trips to Byron, the alternative creative outlet, the seat next to me at the movies, the hugs, the friendship, the true love, the village—all that stuff, too.

But mostly for the horse.

Praise for
Ally Blake

"I found *Hired by the Mysterious Millionaire* by Ally Blake to be a fascinating read... The story of how they get to their HEA is a page-turner. 'Love conquers all' and does so in a very entertaining way in this book."

—*Harlequin Junkie*

PROLOGUE

My desk buzzed.

Or, to be precise, the fancy intercom my gung-ho interior designers had embedded *into* my new desk.

So embroiled had I been in the utterly delightful photographs my private detective had sent me, I might have flinched. Which, as I am nearly seventy-six years of age, could be a health hazard.

My assistant's voice followed, carrying the slightest hint of defeat, as if it wasn't the first time she'd tried to rouse me. "Vivian? Ms Ascot? Your ten o'clock is here."

I swiped crooked fingers over the hidden touchscreen, in search of the appropriate button with which to answer.

"All these new-fangled technologies," I muttered, rolling my eyes at my little dog, Max, who peered up at me from his personal, antique chaise longue beside my office chair. "In the olden days a simple knock at the door sufficed. Yet another sign the world is overtaking me." Then, to my assistant, "And whom might my ten o'clock be?"

A whisper through the speaker, tinged with a hint of hauteur, replied, "The ghost writer."

"Oh! Excellent. Let him up."

I had been approached more than once over the years to write my autobiography. *"Your life!"*

those in charge of such things had expressed. *"Your charitable work! Your support of the arts! A woman—"* gasp! *"—in charge of such a stupendously successful company!"*

But this was the first time I'd entertained the idea. The first time I'd felt as if I had something of worth to share. I was quite looking forward to their shock when they realised it had little to do with my net worth.

Knowing it would take a minute or two for the writer to make it up the lift to my office high atop the Ascot Building in central London, I went back to enjoying the photographs of my lovely young friend, and most recent recipient of the Vivian Ascot Scholarship to Life—a delightful Australian girl named Aubrey Trusedale—arriving safely and stepping off the plane in Rome. First stop on the international adventure my scholarship was funding.

"You remember Aubrey, right, Max?" I said. "And Jessica and Daisy? They are the ones who rescued you when you leapt from my arms at the annual Ascot Music Festival when it was held in Copenhagen. Stopped you from being trampled to death."

Max's delightful little ears pricked. Perhaps at the thought of being trampled to death, but I chose to believe he was remembering the good part. The way those three girls had fawned over him. The way they didn't make me feel silly for being so upset when I thought he'd disappeared for good.

I paused the slide show on one photograph. Sat forward. Squinted. Not sure how much worse my eyes could get before my glass lenses became so heavy they'd make me hunch.

Back when we first met, Aubrey had been a little on the wild side. With a mass of head-turning auburn waves and the trust the world would catch her if she fell. The result—I felt—of having three burly older brothers who adored her to pieces.

As I look at her now, beneath a hat too big for her head, the auburn hair poking out beneath was more a shaggy bob. She seemed a little lankier, too. Chin up, grin plastered across her elfin face as she traipsed through the airport, hands gripped tight to the straps of her battered backpack. All joy, gumption and grit. But changed.

No wonder, after all she'd been through.

I could only hope the infusion of funds from the Vivian Ascot Opportunity Legacy—better? Or too much of a mouthful?—would give her the chance to find her feet again.

"Max," I said, a strange kind of melancholy coming over me, "is it wrong of me to envy her? Not for her youth, or her loveliness, or her excellent eyesight. But for the fact she is about to experience Italy for the first time. The impossibly green hills of Tuscany, the ancient architecture of Rome."

And the men, I said, only this time to myself.

For Max was a sensitive soul. Nowhere else in the world makes men quite like those of Roman blood.

Max's greying muzzle twitched as he looked up at me, limpid brown dachshund eyes a little rheumy, pitying even. I could all but hear him saying, *Vivian, dear, it's not like you to be so schmaltzy.*

Well, he'd feel schmaltzy too, if he was finding himself looking back more than he was looking forward. Such as now, as I found myself drowning in the bittersweet memories of a single summer spent under the Chianti sun.

It was why the Vivian Ascot Endowment Fund for Most Excellent Young Women had been born. Yes, I quite like that one!

The reason I'd endowed those young women with the means to achieve their dream? Instinct.

I couldn't see the future, or sense the lotto numbers, or lead police to dead bodies like that lady on the television. But I could *sense* what people needed, if they needed it enough. Not need as in a little extra deodorant wouldn't go astray. But deeper. Transformative. That one thing that would make a person feel whole.

Whole, I thought, my hand going to my chest. To the strange bittersweet sensation that had taken up residence therein the moment I had seen the first picture of Aubrey in Rome.

I'd been twenty or twenty-one when, in a trattoria in Florence, I'd found myself face to face with the most beautiful man I'd ever met. Tall, dark, Italian. He'd smiled at me, as if he'd known exactly how he'd affected me—

I shook it off.

It was a long time ago. I had no regrets.

I might never have married, or had children of my own, but I'd travelled and laughed and imbibed and inhaled and delighted and felt great wonder. My life was, and had been, wonderful. People wouldn't be throwing so much money my way to hear about it otherwise.

Not that I needed the funds. I had amassed a fortune the likes of which no one person could ever hope to spend. None of which I could leave to Max as I fully planned on outliving my darling boy.

And so the endowments to the lovely Jessica, Daisy and now Aubrey. I had been biding my time, waiting for the right moment to pounce. I mean *help*. Nudge—gently, generously, benignly—towards that which might allow them to shake off the fears holding them back, so that they might truly thrive.

"Ms Ascot," my assistant called through the speaker in my desk. "Your ten o'clock is here."

"Let him in."

The door opened with a soft click and an electronic whir. All this technology really was a bit ridiculous. Just another sign that perhaps my time in the corporate world was coming to its natural end.

"Hi?" the writer called, his head poking around the door. Hand-picked from one of the few glossy magazines still in print, he was young enough the whiskers on his muzzle were golden and sparse. "I mean hello there, Ms Ascot. I mean… Sorry."

I pushed back my chair, moved around the desk, and held out a hand. "Call me Viv."

"Viv," he said. "All right. Though I'm not sure I've ever been quite this star struck."

"Star struck?" I repeated, quite liking that. I gave Max a look, to find he was pretending to be asleep.

"You are *the* Vivian Ascot," the writer intoned, arms spread wide. "Head of Ascot Industries. Benefactor of the Ascot Music Festival. Ascot Music Awards. More galleries and performing arts scholarships and publishing endowments than we likely even know. You, ma'am, are a true patron of the arts."

"You have done your research, young man."

The young man smiled, and I saw a flicker of determination behind the soft face. "Why?" he asked.

"Why do I spend such a large portion of my hard-earned money on pursuits in the arts? Because without art, without beauty and invention and elegance and verve, what is there to live for?"

"No, I mean why do you want to write a book?"

Because I had a story to tell. A story of kindness, and hope, and love.

"Well," I said, "the idea came to me the weekend I met three lovely young women at my music festival in Copenhagen…"

CHAPTER ONE

AUBREY TRUSEDALE HAD imagined this very moment—meeting him for the first time—more times than she could count.

She'd known her fingers would tingle as they did now, imagining how he'd feel to touch. Her blood rushing heedlessly around her body. Heart skittering in her chest. Spotting him across the crowded room; his size, his infamy, his sheer masculine beauty taking her breath fair away.

At over five metres tall, all marble, muscle and might, the David did *not* disappoint.

After around her seventeenth sigh, Aubrey glanced behind her to find the tour group who'd been milling about when she'd arrived had moved on.

Leaving her alone.

With *him*.

Growing up, her three older brothers had had pictures of cars tacked to their bedroom walls. While she'd had notes, sketches, and printouts depicting paintings by Monet and Waterhouse.

But the poster of the David had had pride of place right over her bed.

Yep. A naked man on her wall. Among her mates, it had been quite the coup.

Now, he was so close. This infamous study of

the male form: shadows, indents, veins, muscles, strength, shape… He was honestly the most beautiful thing she had ever seen. If she fell down dead, right here, she'd die happy.

Not that she planned to fall down dead. A lot of clever people had spent the past two years of her life making sure that would not happen any time soon. So, she was pretty determined to stick it out.

Aubrey took a step closer. And another. Till she was all but leaning over the surprisingly small barrier. It wouldn't take much to reach out and touch—

She curled her fingers into her palms.

The number one rule in these places was no touching. Longevity, future generations and all that. But the guy *had* survived outdoors for nearly four hundred years before he was moved into this space.

Would he feel cold? Rough? Dry? Surely a fingertip couldn't hurt. Maybe a gentle sweep of her palm over his—

She glanced over her shoulder to see Mario the security guard strolling by. Heat creeping into her cheeks, she gave him a wave.

Mario grinned back. And hid a yawn behind his hand. He'd worked at the Galleria dell'Accademia for nearly seven years. He had four teenaged daughters. All of whom made it difficult for him to get to sleep at night.

She knew because they'd chatted for a bit when

she'd first stepped inside the gallery doors. People opened up to her. Always had. Made them happy to do things for her. Go the extra mile.

Like the time at the Ascot Music Festival in Copenhagen when she'd first met her very best friends in the entire world, Daisy and Jessica. After rescuing a cheeky little sausage dog from being trampled by thousands of unknowing feet they'd also taken care of Viv—the dog's owner— when it turned out she'd twisted her ankle, badly, in trying to chase little Max down.

While everyone else fretted over Viv, off Aubrey went, found a guy with a golf cart who was meant to be ferrying around VIPS, and convinced him to schlep Viv away to the medical tent instead.

Crazy to think they'd only just this summer discovered that their friend Viv was none other than Vivian Ascot, billionaire head of the Ascot Industries and sponsor of the music festival!

Ask questions, and actually listen to the answers and you never know what might happen. Such as two years later waking up to a legal letter telling you that you had been gifted a bottomless, all-expenses-paid, first-class world trip by that very same billionaire, who would not take oh-my-gosh-you-are-so-lovely-but-I-can't-possibly-accept for an answer.

Something her brothers could learn—the asking, the listening. It was a wonder any woman had married them. Much less had their children. Their gorgeous, roly-poly cherubs. Thinking about how much her beautiful nieces and nephews would grow while she was away had been the one thing that could have stopped her from going.

And yet, some time away from those beautiful babies, all that they represented, all she'd never have, was the very reason she'd had to go.

Realising she was on her tippy toes, Aubrey let herself sway back onto her heels. Consoling herself with the knowledge that the air she breathed had wafted over the David. It was enough. Unless she planned to be arrested for fondling a priceless piece of art before being extradited home on day one of her magical fantasy trip, it had to be.

A couple came into the room, took one look at the David, and kept walking. *Philistines.*

Knowing her one-on-one time with the love of her life was too good to last, Aubrey plonked herself down on the floor, stretched open her backpack, pulled out a sketch pad and the stub of a fine charcoal pencil, looked back up at the David, and breathed.

Which bit to sketch first? That dashing profile? The whorl of his ear? His foot—the one that had lost a toe when some crazy had chopped it off with a hammer?

The hand.

It was his fault she'd always had a thing for

hands. Strong hands. With veins and scars and strength and a story.

Aubrey stared at the David's hand for another few seconds before putting pencil to paper. With a sweep of charcoal across the page, there was no going back.

Drawing had always been her bliss. Sketching with a stick in the dirt in their hot, dry inner Sydney backyard, using her toe to create sand animals on their biannual trips to the beach. It had been a way to escape into her head when she'd needed time out from her boisterous family of six.

First money she'd made had been as a precocious eight-year-old, setting herself up on the sidewalk outside her family's Sydney auto shop, Prestige Panel and Paint, selling pictures she'd drawn of the vintage cars inside. She'd put the money in a tin she'd marked *Plane Ride*.

Resolute, even then, to see the world.

Her dream had seemed ill-starred, when, two years earlier, while finally on the trip she'd saved for her entire life, just after the Copenhagen festival, she'd been cut down by a mysterious infection that doctors had told her family would most certainly be the end of her.

Realising her pencil had stopped moving, Aubrey blinked to clear her eyes, then tipped her dad's old fedora further back on her head and smudged a little graphite shadow into a groove of David's wrist with her thumb.

It *hadn't* been the end of her. She'd pulled through. After two long years of obstinate recuperation, she was back. Only now she carried with her one slightly damaged heart.

She looked up at the David—*the David*, right there in front of her—and thanked whatever gods out there might have helped pull her through. Asking them if they could stick around, keep an eye on her, make sure nothing happened to force her home too soon this time.

Not that she believed it would. This time things seemed fortuitous, sprinkled as they were with Vivian Ascot's particular brand of magical fairy dust. The timing could not have been more perfect, coming as it had right on top of the most recent bombshell from Aubrey's doctors.

When Viv had stated—tongue in cheek, Aubrey was almost sure—that the only provisos were that she was not to deny herself a thing, that she luxuriate and spoil herself rotten, and that she start her trip in Florence, staying in a hotel Viv herself owned, what choice had she had but to accept?

Dante. Machiavelli. Da Vinci. Michelangelo. Galileo. Of the greats, only a small number were born in Florence or spent time there. If this trip was to be Aubrey's renaissance, her chance to envision her life beyond her condition, and all it had taken from her, this was the city to do it.

"I don't know about you," a deep, male voice

said from behind her, "but he's always bigger than I think he'll be."

Aubrey flinched and the charcoal slipped, leaving a bold black streak right across the page.

"Well, poo," she said.

"Whoa, sorry," the voice said. Australian, she realised. How funny was that?

Aubrey shrugged. Mishaps were a part of the story. They did not define it. "No worries. It's hardly a Rembrandt."

Shadow fell over her as the owner of the voice moved in, blocking the light pouring into the room from the huge glass dome above as he looked over her shoulder. "No," he said. "But it's damn good."

Aubrey held onto her hat and turned. Looked up. And…hot damn.

Talk about bigger than you expected! It was difficult not to gawp. For the man was tall. Built. Dark chocolate hair raked into devastatingly sexy spikes. Sunglasses hooked into the collar of his pale grey T-shirt that did little to hide the shape beneath. The man behind the voice was handsome enough to have her blush, just a little, as big, handsome guys always had.

"Thanks," she said with a quick smile, shoving her stuff back in her vintage backpack, yanking the frayed leather strap around the opening to tighten it up. She slung it over her shoulder and got back to her feet as gracefully as possible, which in short overalls and floppy sandals wasn't graceful at all.

"You sketch the big guy a lot?" asked Mr Tall Dark and Aussie, his gaze roaming around the big room.

He'd moved away again. Not crowding her. *Handsome and thoughtful,* she thought. *Nice.* Nice and big and beautiful, with a nose Michelangelo would have wept over, a hard jawline, and lips she'd kill to sketch.

"First time," she said, blinking ten to the dozen when his gaze moved back her way. "But it won't be the last, I hope. He's magnificent. Bucket-list stuff, right there."

"Hmm," the stranger hummed. The deep sound seeming to reverberate through Aubrey's chest.

"You don't agree?"

"Me? No. He's…fine."

Aubrey tried not to sputter. "*Fine?* He's perfection."

That earned her a raised eyebrow. If anything, it made the stranger even more ridiculously gorgeous. Her toes curled into her sandals.

"Marble's not my medium," he said, his gaze on the statue looming anciently over them.

"What is?"

"Wood."

At that, Aubrey tried not to look at David's bits. She really did. But with the stranger's declaration bouncing about inside her head, and David's bits staring back at her three times normal size… She was only human.

"Intimidated?" she asked, her cheeks tugging into a smile.

There was a moment, a beat that felt like a thud deep inside her chest, before his eyes narrowed. Then he lifted his chin and said, "Nah."

"Ha!"

At her bark of laughter, he swung his eyes her way. And the last of her breath left her lungs in a whoosh. His eyes were ridiculous. Deep blue, and dark and mysterious, like a river at night. Eyes a girl could drown in.

She'd use a well-sharpened pencil if she sketched him. Or a fine black pen. She'd need to get the sweep of each individual eyelash just right. The defined angle of his jaw. The chiselled curve of that seriously enticing mouth.

And those eyes, the flash of blue that might well turn a piercing aquamarine out in the sunshine, the thought of studying them enough to do them justice, made her feel light in the head.

In accepting Viv's generous gift, Aubrey had made herself a promise. To use this amazing opportunity to find a new normal, now that the future she'd always believed would be hers could not be.

No time like the present to begin.

She held out a hand to the most beautiful—

flesh and blood——man she had ever seen and said, "Aubrey Trusedale. Of Sydney."

A beat later, he took it. Said, "Malone. Sean Malone." No qualification as to where he'd hailed from. *Melbourne,* she thought, taking in the cut of his clothes. The effortless style. *Definitely Melbourne.*

Taking a pause seemed to be a thing for him. A moment in which to make a decision. Find the most famous statue of a naked man in the world intimidating, or not. Talk to the strange girl, or not.

When the heat from Sean Malone's hand spread into hers, the unexpected calluses on the pads of his palms rubbing against the matching ones on hers, she smiled. And meant it.

"I'm very glad to have met you, Malone."

A half-hour later, Sean found himself unsure as to how he'd ended up in the Piazza Della Signoria having a coffee with a stranger he'd picked up along the way.

Or had she picked him up?

One of them had mentioned being starving, which, on reflection, didn't sound like him.

So here he was, sweltering beneath a bright yellow sun umbrella, at a rickety wrought-iron table, palming a cooling espresso, and packed in like a sardine with a zillion other sun-baskers doing the same.

While she—the stranger, Aubrey Trusedale of Sydney—was leaning over the back of her chair, chatting with the South African couple at the next table about their travels—and jobs, and families, and favourite books—leaving Sean to wait, and muse, and remember.

None of which he was keen to do.

But first… "Aubrey."

She held up a staying finger. "Just a sec."

Sean held out a hand in supplication, but nobody was paying him any heed.

So, he leaned around the table and grabbed the woman's backpack. It was wide open. Without even trying to see inside he spotted paper, pens, wallet, sunglasses, what looked like spare clothes in a Ziploc bag, and a lacy G-string sitting right on top.

He pulled the strap that scrunched the bag closed— mostly, the thing was built for pilfering—before squeezing the bag between the table leg and his own.

And waited. And mused. And remembered.

Having lived in Florence near on five years now he'd visited the David more than once, but playing tourist had *not* been how he'd planned to start his day.

The email. The email had knocked him off course.

Once his team had arrived at the workshop he'd built beneath his place in the hills overlooking the city, the sounds of saws and music spilling through the open windows, he'd walked out of the front door. Leaving his dog at the villa, for the day was far too hot to lug Elwood down the hill.

The height of summer had descended over Florence, bringing with it the usual humidity and plague of tourists, so by the time he'd hit the city his head was no clearer. The answer to the email still unformed.

So he'd kept walking. Meandering the back streets; lean, shadowed caverns between the old stone buildings it was easy to get lost in. It was what he'd loved most about the city. He'd lost himself there years ago.

And he'd found himself outside the Galleria dell'Accademia—its unassuming wooden door tucked into the side of an unending row of beige buildings—as the sun had truly begun to burn.

Taking a break from the heat, he'd gone in. Made his way to the most famous artefact in the place, and found her sitting there—Aubrey Trusedale of Sydney—cross-legged, in the middle of the gallery floor.

Short overalls over a white T-shirt covered in faces of black cats, one strap half falling off her shoulder. Sandals only just clinging to her feet. Her back to the room. Her backpack on the floor beside her, wide open.

He could have moved on. Kept walking. Made his way back to the air-conditioned bliss of his city showroom. Answered the email and moved on with his life.

But something about the way her shoe had been half falling off, and her hat was too big for her head, had made him stop.

Florence was a great city, but like any city—any place—bad things could happen. And something about her screamed trouble magnet.

Not that he had a knight-in-shining-armour complex. He intentionally kept out of other people's business and appreciated them doing the same for him. But the bag—he had to say something. Only when he'd moved in did he notice she was sketching.

Her fingers had gripped so tight to a charcoal pencil her knuckles had gone white, and yet the sweep of movement over the paper—it had been arresting. Her style loose and easy. The lines bold yet graceful.

She was very good.

He'd have recognised the subject anywhere. The David's right hand. Famously larger than it ought to have been. Supposedly a nod to the man's inner strength. Though it messed with Sean's architectural brain.

A bespoke furniture designer by trade, he sketched all the time. Mostly on grid paper—straight lines and precise curves. Shapes he could build. Shapes that were comfortable to the eye.

And the backside. Shapes that had people on wait lists for his designs.

Yet he had none of her light hand. None of her sense of freedom. Her effortless speed. And he'd found himself entranced.

He'd watched her pencil fly over the page for a full minute before he'd heard a voice. Surprised to find it was his own.

Then she'd looked up at him. All big brown Bambi eyes. Eyes full of spark. Eyes that had taken one look at him and warmed all over. Clear that she'd liked what she'd seen, and that she'd had no ability—or, perhaps, intention—of hiding it.

Only then had come the accent. Australian.

Of all the days...

For the email that had sent him walking had been from back home. Hidden, innocently, between the usual—invitations to gallery openings, to guest lecture at tech schools and museums, to present a TED talk, even a nudge to see if he might be keen to co-host a renovation show on British TV.

The email was a commission enquiry for a custom memorabilia shelving unit for a pre-eminent Australian Rules Football club.

It wasn't his usual thing. His custom pieces tended to be more specialised. Twelve-foot doors. Monolithic tables. In the past year he'd been called on to build a throne. His sister used to call this sideline of his vocation Shock and Awe.

Sean blinked at the vision of his sister's face, blaming the damn email anew. Then downed the last of his coffee, holding onto the bitter aftertaste.

The email had been sent by a friend of his father.

His father whom he hadn't seen in half a decade. Hadn't spoken to in, what, a year? More? Was it a coincidence? Or could it be his old man's way of reaching out?

Laughter brought him back to the now.

A waiter had joined in the conversation on the other side of the table. Telling a story, in broken English, that had Aubrey and her new friends in stitches. The young man held a menu in what looked to be a most uncomfortable position, high above his head so that it stopped a shard of sunlight between the umbrella edges from hitting Aubrey in the face.

Mid smile, she reached for her bag. Found it missing. She spun on her chair, Bambi eyes wide.

Sean lifted the bag and passed it over the table.

And her eyes met his. Direct. Warm. Zesty. Filled with laughter and suggestion and temptation. Heat swept over him—inevitable and true. Heat that had nothing to do with the bite of the summer's day.

She fixed the strap of her overalls that had slipped off one shoulder. Mouthed, *Thank you*. Then ferreted around inside the bag till she grabbed what looked like a mint and tossed it back with the last of her coffee.

She paused mid swallow as she caught his eye again; this time her expression was far more guarded. She ran a finger over her lips and said, "Special vitamins."

He nodded. Waited for her to turn back to her new friends. And breathed out.

That was how he'd ended up here.

Back in the gallery, her eyes on his, head cocked, her hat slipping off her head to reveal short, shaggy auburn waves. Freckles on a fine nose. Dark smudges beneath those warm, inviting eyes. Lips that might seem too wide for such a delicate face, unless a person had seen them smile.

The squeeze of her hand reminding him he hadn't let her go.

"Is it just me," she'd said, "or do you also feel the urge to jump over that little fence and touch the big guy?"

After a moment Sean had shaken his head.

"It's like a current running under my skin. You really don't feel it too?"

He'd felt something. Concern, he'd told himself, at the fact her backpack now slowly eased open as she jumped from foot to foot, energised by that current under her skin.

"Maybe I'm just hungry. Do you know a place?"

And here they were.

Across the table Aubrey said goodbye to her

new friends and turned to him, her expression chagrined. "Sorry, they were about to leave for Rome this afternoon and hadn't seen the David. I felt like it was my mission to convince them they must."

"Success?" he asked.

"Success," she said, those wide lips stretching into a huge smile. Then she dropped her hands to the table, leaned forward and said, "So, now what?"

Her focus was sharp. Her smile encouraging. And for a second Sean felt as if the current she'd spoken about flickered deep inside him.

He lifted his hands deliberately from the table and pushed back his chair. "Now I have work to do. What are your plans?"

The edge of her smile dropped, but she rallied quickly. "You know what, I'm exhausted. I think I'll head back to my hotel, get a good night's sleep and start anew tomorrow."

"Lead the way."

"It wasn't an invitation for you to join me there," she said over her shoulder as they threaded their way through the tightly packed tables, the glint in her eyes making it clear she was joking.

"I'm aware."

"Are you sure? I wouldn't want to hurt your feelings."

"My feelings are just fine."

"I mean, we've only just met. And you aren't a

fan of the David. And this is my first day in town so I really should keep my options open."

Hands in pockets, Sean followed. "Sounds like a good plan."

Sean would escort her back to whatever back-packer place she was booked into and on the way he'd give her some sage advice on the areas to avoid. Recommend she ditch the backpack and simplify what she needed to take out with her into the streets.

And feel safe in the knowledge he'd done all he could to make sure a stranger he'd once met lived through the day.

Aubrey fell back on the lush king-sized bed in her opulent suite.

Viv had made it very clear that she was not al-lowed to take a single cent back to Australia with her. That it all had to be spent. On luxury accom-modation and gastronomical feasts, on gondola rides and hot-air balloons and helicopter flights and every sensory experience a person could pos-sibly imagine.

Aubrey closed her eyes, breathing in the sin-gular scent—like snow and freesias and spun gold—and replayed every second of her first day in Florence.

Firenze. The city of flowers. Of Machiavelli and the Medicis. Of Michelangelo and Rembrandt. The freaking David!

And Sean Malone.

She wriggled on the bed, the current she'd felt under her skin in the gallery back with a vengeance. She'd assumed it was due to the man on the stand. Maybe it had more than a little to do with the real live one instead.

She bit her lip to stop from grinning.

Who'd have thought? First day and she'd already met some tall, dark handsome stranger, had a coffee with the guy, while a statue of a Medici on horseback looked over them, and a fountain depicting Neptune and a bunch of seahorses bubbled ostentatiously in the background.

It had been an overload of sensation. The warmth on her skin. The effusive banter in Italian, flowing and tripping all around her. The smooth dark flavour of the coffee.

She might have pinched herself. Twice.

Despite the jet lag and her usual fatigue tugging at the corners of her subconscious, she sat up, bounced her way to the end of the huge bed, and grabbed her phone. Hoping somewhere in the world one of her friends would be awake.

The first to answer the video chat was Jessica. Diligent to the last.

"Aubrey!" she said, rubbing her eyes and yawning.

"Oh, no. Did I wake you?"

"Hmm? No, it's fine. I must have fallen asleep on the couch. We were watching *When Harry Met*

Sally. Jamie and I are on week two of a New York rom-com binge."

Aubrey's eyebrows lifted. "He agreed to that? Jeez. He really must be love struck."

Jessica attempted to glare but she was way too sweet, and way too in *lurve* to pull it off. "Tell me, what's happening in Aubrey land?"

Aubrey lifted the phone, twirled it slowly about the insanely glamorous suite Viv had put her up in, then carried the phone to the window, pulling back the floaty curtains to show off her view. The Arno river. The Ponte Vecchio. The buttery sunshine pouring over the ancient architecture.

"Oh, my gosh!" Jess's voice came through the speaker. Then a little muffled, as she turned away, to talk over her shoulder. "It's Aubrey. She's in Florence."

"Hey, Aubs." That was Jamie. Jessica's wonderful new suit-and-tie guy.

Aubrey had spoken to him a handful of times since he and Jessica had fallen for one another and she loved him already. For Jessica. He wasn't *her* type. Too straight up and down. Too smitten.

Aubrey wouldn't turn down the chance for a little romance while on her trip, a fast and fiery meeting of the souls—but until she figured out what the next phase of her life would look like she wasn't dragging some poor love-struck guy into the picture.

"Hey, Jamie!" she said, moving to sit on the

floor, leaning against the velvet banquette at the end of her bed. "How's it hanging? Or should I ask Jessica when you're out of the room?"

The wide-eyed look he gave her matched Jessica's to a T. Made for one another, those two.

"Have fun, Aubs," he said before heading out of shot.

"Planning on it!" Aubrey called, her voice echoing in her massive suite.

Jessica's face returned; she was biting her bottom lip to stop from laughing. "So tell me. What have you been up to so far? Eaten your weight in pasta? Accidentally touched any great works of art? Fallen in lust with the man of your dreams?"

Sean Malone's handsome face slid into her subconscious, and Aubrey's heart shifted. Or squeezed. It moved in a way she was not used to, and wasn't looking for. She had a love-hate relationship with the reliability of that particular organ. She gave her chest a bump with her fist, told it to settle down.

The shock must have shown in her face, as Jessica's brow knitted a moment before she rolled her eyes. "I meant the *David*! Did you get to see the David?"

"Oh! Right." Aubrey laughed, letting her hand fall away from her chest. "And yes. Yes!"

She crawled over to her backpack—a gorgeous, deep, soft, vintage-green suede thing she'd bought online that looked as well travelled as she one day wished she would be. Sure, it didn't close all that well, which Mr Malone had mentioned more than once as he'd walked her home, but it had the perfect inner pockets for wallet, phone, wipes, spare clothes, passport and, most importantly, her meds.

She scrounged around till she found her sketchbook, turned to the page where she'd sketched the David's hand, with its raw, angled knuckles and beautiful roping veins. She held the picture up to the phone.

"Wow, Aubrey," Jessica breathed. "Just…wow. Jamie! Come see what our girl drew!"

As she flipped through the pages for her captive audience, she found herself imagining the hand turned to flesh. Tanned, male, brute strength evident in the curl of the fingers as they rested loosely around an espresso glass. Short square nails, dark stains in the creases of his knuckles. Not dirt. Oil? Varnish? And scars. Several scars.

She remembered the feel of that hand wrapped around hers. The heat humming beneath the surface. The rough calluses creating an echo, a scraping sensation, in her belly.

"Aubrey?" Jessica's voice drifted into her subconscious. "Aubs?"

Daisy's voice joined in. "Is she okay? She looks flushed. Why are you flushed? Are you okay?"

Aubrey dropped the sketchbook and her hands flew to her cheeks to find them warm. Dammit.

The last thing she needed was the girls worrying about her. On day one!

"Daisy!" she said, leaning forward and flapping her hands at the small camera. Distraction was one of her better skills. "Oh, my gosh, is that rock star Daisy Mulligan?"

Daisy rolled her eyes. "Are you okay?"

"I'm fine. Fabulous. It's just a zillion degrees here. I've been out, absorbing fresh air and sunshine."

"How was the flight?" Daisy asked, eyes narrowed.

"The flight. Was that today?" Jessica asked. "Must be an awfully long flight from Australia. Make sure you rest."

"Any time you can," Daisy added.

"Mum. Dad," Aubrey said. "You can stop fussing now."

Both of her friends cringed.

"Sorry," said Daisy, resting her chin on her hand till her lovely face was squashed. "Tell us about the hot city-boy Italians. I missed that being out in the country. Do they *ooze* sex appeal? Can you walk straight what with your trembling loins?"

Aubrey glanced to Jessica's face on the other half of the screen and pointed her thumb at Daisy. "You'd never believe she writes hit lyrics for a living."

Jessica laughed. "Don't change the subject."

"Okay, fine! The guard watching over the David's name is Mario. He has four daughters and occasional gout."

"She's trying to distract us," Daisy muttered to Jessica.

"I concur," Jessica said. "Meaning she's holding something back."

Aubrey loved her friends dearly. Even though they lived in different parts of the world, they were so close. They could open up about things, fears, failings, in ways they couldn't to those closest by. Or maybe that was why. But sometimes she kind of wished they didn't know her so well.

"Okay, fine. But I'll need vocal lubrication for this." Aubrey took her phone to the tiny pod-coffee machine by the window and made herself an espresso. Over the whir she told them about Sean Malone.

When she finished she waited for the good-natured ribbing. But while Jessica looked doe-eyed, Daisy appeared furious.

"We said she should have done a tour," said Daisy. "Stayed with a group. Had a buddy. Been on a list that had to be checked off hourly. She's too trusting."

"Far too trusting," Jessica conceded, blinking away the romance in her eyes.

"Is that what you were wearing?" Daisy asked.

Aubrey glanced down at the white T-shirt covered in black cats she wore under her shortie denim overalls. "Jessica gave it to me last Christmas."

"Exactly!" sad Daisy, as if that proved the fact that Aubrey should not be let out of the house alone. "What if he's some kind of weirdo? A stalker? A...predator?"

"You think?" said Jessica. "He did take her out for coffee."

"Hello!" Aubrey called, drawing focus. "I'm right here. Sean Malone did not take me out for coffee. I drank coffee. He drank coffee. We sat on opposite sides of the same table. And he pretty much spent every spare moment telling me how to stay safe."

That was right. The conversation hadn't been at all romantic, come to think of it. He'd given her the rundown on tourism safety while she'd nattered on about all the things she planned to do on this trip.

But not the why. People always turned weird when they found out she'd been so sick. Her body so scourged she'd had to relearn how to walk. Her joints sore. Her muscles weakened. Much of her long curly auburn hair had fallen out. Her mother had cried when, a year ago, she'd shaved it off.

Another reason she loved her girls so much. They thought she was just as fierce and fabulous now as in the Before. Which was why they wanted her to pace herself. They knew it wasn't her nature.

"He told me how to hide my money and papers under my clothes."

"He did what?" Daisy shot back.

"*Told* me. Not showed me. Jeez." Though the thought of those hands sliding up under her shirt, or tugging at the beltline of her shorts, was not a terrible one.

"Well, that sounds nice," said Jessica aka Miss Always Look on the Bright Side. "Not stalkerish at all."

"Yep. Just a nice Australian guy, helping another Australian." So why did that make Aubrey suddenly feel as if she'd run over a nail with fresh new tyres?

"What was his name again?" Daisy asked.

"Malone," Aubrey said distractedly. "Sean Malone."

"And he's Australian. Why is that name familiar?" Daisy brought up her phone, thumbs flying over the screen. "I've been reading a lot of true crime of late."

When Daisy's eyes went wide, Aubrey had a pretty good idea she'd found him. Daisy held up her phone. "This him?"

One look at the swish of dark hair, the chiselled jaw, the lovingly carved lips, the deeply romantic blue eyes burning into the camera and Aubrey felt her cheeks go hot once more. "Mm hmm."

"Whoa," said Daisy. "He's—"

"I know, right?" Aubrey breathed.

"I mean he's really really…"

"Gorgeous," they said in tandem.

Then they laughed, and any tension that had been there as a result of her favourite girls looking out for her just a little too much dissipated.

"Says here he's a well-respected furniture maker. Born in Melbourne. Based in Florence."

"So he *lives* here."

"Has for several years, it seems. He's kind of famous, actually. His stuff has ended up in houses of movie stars, presidential meeting rooms, a palace or three. His medium is wood—tables, chairs, fancy architectural stuff—oh, my God! That's where I know him from! My Jay has a couple of his chairs, big manly beastly things, all square arms and leather seats, he wanted to bring to the cottage till we realised they wouldn't fit through the doors. Well, there you go!"

Jessica and Aubrey let Daisy's super-sweet "my Jay" comment go. For all that she was super well-known now, she was deeply private and had a tendency to go underground if she felt cornered.

"Wood," said Aubrey suddenly, as Sean's comment from earlier suddenly made sense. She laughed out loud. Laughed until she felt breathless.

"Okay," said Jessica, "I don't care if I sound like your mother, I think it's time we let you get some rest."

Daisy glared into the camera. "Check in whenever you can so we know you're making good choices."

"Not a chance! Love you guys!"

"Love you too, you terror," said Daisy before signing off.

"Enjoy yourself," said Jessica. "Soak up every second. Just… Take it from me, and I'm sure Daisy would say the same, while Viv's gifts have been life-altering, they can come with a sting in the tail. And after all you've been through, the last thing we want is for you to find yourself stung. Again. So, take care, okay?"

Aubrey nodded. "Promise."

When they both signed off Aubrey let go of a long slow breath.

And the exhaustion she'd been holding at bay came over her in a wave so strong she had to sit. The travel, the heat, the sensory overload, the David, and the guy. It was a lot for one day. A lot for a girl from the suburbs whose highlights from the past two years had been getting the doctor's permission to have butter on her movie popcorn and being given the green light to drive again.

While meeting the likes of Sean Malone had been unexpected, to all intents and purposes, he was as real to her as a marble statue.

And that was okay.

Aubrey crept back onto the bed, the hotel room such a perfect temperature she didn't need to crawl beneath the blankets. She simply curled up in a ball, her head sinking onto the downy pillow.

While her eyes began to flutter, she scrolled

through old folders on her phone till she found the last photo taken of her before she'd fallen ill.

She was holding her phone at the end of her outstretched arm, auburn curls tumbling over her shoulders, cheeks fuller than they were now, a huge grin on her face. Behind her, on the hospital bed, sat one Vivian Ascot. Beside Viv, Jessica and Daisy. Max the dog's little face peeked out from inside Aubrey's jacket.

On a whim she texted the photo to the girls. And then also to Vivian Ascot.

Then she sent a few quick Proof of Life pics to her family. A selfie with the David. The view from her room. The table at the café, with its glossy cappuccinos and red checked tablecloth, one Sean Malone cropped out of shot. A photo of one of her sketches.

She let her phone drop to the bed and closed her eyes.

Seconds later she was out like a light.

CHAPTER TWO

AUBREY DRAGGED ONE eye open, then the other, to find herself face up in a big soft bed; a fresco of a dozen naked cherub babies with wings hovering high above.

The sight of their chubby little legs gave her a massive twinge, right in the ovaries. Meaning it took her a few extra seconds to remember where the heck she was.

She rubbed her eyes, rolled over and sat on the edge of the bed. Through the gap in the gauzy curtains leading out to her balcony, her gaze settled on the sight of Ponte Vecchio, one of the most famous bridges in the world, right outside her window.

And it all came back to her.

Viv's exorbitant gift. Convincing her parents, her doctors, herself that she *had* to take it. The lo-o-o-ong, exhausting flight. Landing in Italy on a sweltering summer's day. The three-hour drive from Rome to Florence with a driver who did not seem to know how to use his brakes—

And, the David. Her life-long crush. In all his marble glory.

Feeling much better about the world and all things in it, Aubrey tipped down onto the floor, padded to the coffee machine and booted it up.

Yawning as the coffee poured, hot and dark, into her glass.

And, as she had done every day for the past year and a half, she checked in with herself. Hand over her heart, eyes closed, as her psychologist had taught her. She waited till she felt her heart beat. Even and sure.

Next her fingers. No numbness. Her legs were a little worn out. A slight ache behind her eyes. Not surprising considering her last couple of days and the amount of things she'd jammed into them. It was a lot, even for a normal person.

Perhaps heading out into the heat to explore the moment she'd reached the hotel hadn't been the smartest choice.

She pictured her mother, hands wringing out a kitchen rag, eyes on the mobile phone propped in the stand her oldest grandchild had made at kindy. Her brothers pacing by their phones, waiting for Proof of Life. Her father, working at the auto shop, pretending he wasn't laying a hand on the phone attached to his tool belt with a clip she'd painted, so he wouldn't miss the buzz.

Should she stay in for a day? Recoup her energy? Rethink her beautiful vintage backpack as Sean had suggested, while she was at it?

"Oh," she said, the word catching in her throat, as Sean Malone came back to her in a whumph.

Grumpy, bossy, quite famous furniture builder

and all around hot guy. Imagine if she'd stayed in the day before and missed that?

Question answered, she squared her shoulders. Grabbed her phone. Took a quick photo of her view and added it to the family chat with the message My view is better than yours! then tossed her phone onto her bed and padded to the bathroom, which was bigger than her apartment back home.

Showered and dressed, with her vintage backpack over her shoulder, she headed out into the beautiful summer's day.

If she couldn't run with the bulls, or drink herself under the table, or boldly touch a piece of art that connected her to centuries of masters who subsumed themselves to the wonder of beauty, then what was the point in dreaming big at all?

She just had to find a way to do all that, while not wearing herself to collapse, before her world tour had barely begun.

And she knew just where to start.

Sean sipped on an espresso, his elbows leaning on the countertop in his showroom in the Via Alighieri, his mind a million miles away.

Or, to be precise, a couple of hundred metres away, where, on the opposite bank of the Arno River, stood the Florentine Hotel where he'd left one Aubrey Trusedale the afternoon before.

The Florentine was no backpacker joint. It was

six-star, with views of the Ponte Vecchio and across to the Pitti Palace. What a girl in cut-off overalls and flappy sandals was doing staying in a place like that, on her own so far as he could tell, was a mystery.

A mystery he had no intention of spending another moment concerning himself with after he'd done all he could the day before to send her safely on her way. And yet, here he was, spending moments. Plural. Thinking about those warm, unfiltered, golden brown eyes.

But it was either that, or stew over the email from back home. The one he'd yet to answer.

Through the cracks in the stone walls Sean could hear the faint echo of applause from the ten o'clock tour group, no doubt packed to the rafters watching the leather-stamping display in Bella Pelle next door.

Distraction. That was what he needed. Noise, not quiet. Not time inside his own head.

He moved around the counter, boots scuffing the ancient mosaic floor, and Elwood lifted his smooth silvery head, solemn blue Weimaraner eyes looking at Sean.

"Walk?"

The dog's chin slid back to the floor.

"Maybe later."

Sean propped open the glass door, using a wooden wedge—an offcut from a table he'd made years ago. The summer air hit like a furnace blast, tendrils leaking around him into the air-conditioned comfort beyond.

Summer in Florence was a testament to the city's draw; the heat enough to make a person squint, but not enough to turn them away.

Leaning in the doorway, letting the Italian sun thaw him out, he hoped the heat, the noise, the colour, the life outside his door would burn away the thoughts that refused to clear.

Turned out half the proprietors in the laneway were doing the same; leaning in their shopfront doorways, eyes on the street as it thrummed under the weight of the summer tourist infestation.

Enzo, the restaurateur, called out the daily specials to those who wandered by. Offered free wine, free garlic bread, free hugs. A couple of people took the hugs, more still fell for his charm and found themselves swept inside.

Gia, the leathersmith, shooed the tour group out of the door, while wiping a hand across her brow.

Roberto, the jeweller, was no Enzo on the charm front, but his wares were inducement enough. The man was a true artisan. He even had another shop on the Ponte Vecchio itself.

Sean knew their stories. They were vocal about their successes. And their heartaches. For they were a bold bunch; effusive, emotional, happy to be all up in one another's space.

But they did not know him. Or his story. Polite

hellos. Discussions about the weather. That was his limit. He didn't do sharing. It was not his way. Not here. not any more.

"Gian!" called Enzo, snapping his checked tea towel over one shoulder. "You look hungry! What can I bring you?"

Sean shook his head, and lifted his espresso glass to show he was good.

Enzo scoffed. "I'll bring you *tiramisù*. Or *cassata* Siciliana…*panna cotta…babà…tartufo di Pizzo…*"

It was a play they had acted out so many times he could recite it by heart. Enzo trying gamely to feed him, the Italian way of bringing someone into the fold. And Sean resisting.

"I'm fine," Sean called, stepping back as a group of young female tourists scurried close, giggling behind their hands.

"Ah, you hurt me. You really do," Enzo cried, all drama, before turning his decidedly unscathed attentions to the paying customers.

No one came to Sean's door. His spot was a display case rather than a shopfront. A stage on which to show examples of his team's more esoteric pieces. The current range his most daring and difficult yet—chairs and coffee tables made of wood warped and shaped in flowing, twisting lines that had them appear as if made of ribbon. Some simplified form of which would soon trickle down into his wholesale lines.

But more than that, it was a place to get away to when the energy of the workshop became too much. Just as the workshop was a place to get away to when the energy of the street circled too close, his life a constant balancing act of punishing work, and solitude.

When Roberto the jeweller looked as if he was building up enough steam to hurtle himself through the crowd and across the laneway, Sean pressed himself away from the doorframe. "Elwood," he said with a whistle. "Time for a walk."

Elwood huffed, then unfolded himself from his spot beneath the air-conditioning vent and lolloped to the door. Sean grabbed and pocketed a lead. Dogs, by law, were free to roam in the city but the Australian in him was too strong to go so far as to take Elwood into a café, or a museum.

He locked up—the cool lighting in the showroom permanently on—then spun out into the lane only to run smack bang into someone coming the other way.

Arms flailed.

Elwood barked.

The stranger swore rather magnificently in English, then dropped to a crouch, collecting sunglasses, hat, bag and any number of things that had gone flying.

Sean froze. Something about the top of the head—the short, shaggy auburn waves—looked familiar.

"Aubrey?"

She looked up, while shoving things inside her ill-advised backpack before attempting to drag its fallible opening closed.

"Malone? Is that—? Oh, my. Hi!" Big, liquid brown eyes beamed up at him. The colour of unstained cherry wood. The colour of home.

Elwood sat on his foot, tail wagging as he panted gently up at their interloper, and when Aubrey caught the dog's eye she lit up, leaning down to ruffle Elwood's ears. "Oh, hello! Aren't you beautiful? Such a good boy. And a *big* boy! Whoa!"

She laughed, all easy grace as she got a nose to the crotch.

"Jeez, Malone," she laughed. "Your dog's a little fresh. I wonder where he learned that move."

Before he could hope to respond, out of the corner of his eye, Sean noted that they had an audience. His fellow vendors were no longer trying to out shout one another. They all hovered in their shopfronts, watching. Patently intrigued by the fact he had a visitor. Or a customer. Or that he was engaging in conversation at all.

Aubrey stood, her eyes finding his once more. "How funny is this? You and me, finding one another again while I was out and about following my feet and… Hang on a sec. My phone!" Aubrey spun on the spot, smacking at her right butt cheek, eyes frantic.

Sean found it beneath Elwood's wagging tail, face down, the case detailed with a photo of what looked like a heart made out of stained glass. Looking closer, he saw it had been painted onto the hood of a muscle car.

He turned it to make sure the screen wasn't damaged, to find the phone on, open to the map. A little red pin pointing right at his showroom.

Following her feet, was she? A muscle flickered in his cheek as he handed the phone over. He watched her eyes widen as she realised she'd been sprung.

"Okay, fine," she said, "I wasn't following my feet. I was kind of stalking you."

"Stalking me."

Out of the corner of his eye, Sean saw Gina hustle over to Enzo, and stage whisper "stalker" while pointing his way. Enzo nodded effusively, as if that made far more sense than him having an actual acquaintance.

"Well, my friend looked you up online, you see," Aubrey was saying. "My other friend is too nice to do that kind of thing. She's Canadian. We kind of drag her along for the ride."

Sean opened his mouth to ask what on earth she was talking about, then thought better of it. The way her eyes moved over his face, the sigh in her voice, transparent, unbridled, he had a pretty good feeling what her conversations with her friends might have entailed.

Aubrey spun to watch an older woman on a Vespa curl in and out of the crowd meandering down the centre of the alley. Her face was bright, alive, as she said, "This place is wild. Crumbling yet posh. You know?"

Figuring it better not to indulge her, he said, "Were you stalking me for a reason?"

She caught his eye, and blinked. "Surely one doesn't stalk a person on a whim."

He lifted an eyebrow and waited.

Eventually she puffed out a surrendering breath. "Okay, then. Here's the truth. Since you're the only person I know in this city, I was hoping you might be able to point me in the direction of a chaperone."

"A chaperone?"

"What? No. Not a *chaperone*. Pfft. I'm a grown woman living in the twenty-first century."

She cocked a hip.

"Look, I hate even asking, because I *am* a grown woman living in the twenty-first century. But I'm here on my own. And while that *was* my plan, to do this trip alone, to own it, you know, to follow my curiosity and soak in every ounce of adventure that fell my way without having to ask permission, it was actually kind of nice, yesterday, having someone to hang with. Someone to remind me to stop and have a cuppa rather than go go go till I collapse."

She waited for him to respond. But he had nothing. Whatever she was asking he was the exact wrong person to ask.

"I don't have a natural off switch, you see," she went on, rocking from foot to foot now, her energy levels ramping up. "Which is totally part of my charm. But Florence is my very first stop. I'm in this travel thing for the long haul, and I don't think packing my days quite so full is a recipe for longevity."

When she looked at him, beseeching him to say something so she could stop, Sean ran a hand up the back of his neck, and glanced down the laneway. "Do you need me to hook you up with a tour company? Gia, next door, the leathersmith, has a lot of groups go through her door."

Aubrey stopped her swaying, and gave him a look that was both direct and shrewd. "You know what? Forget it. I don't know what I want, clearly, and you shouldn't be the one to figure it out for me. Just because we're both Australian, and you clearly find me delightful, doesn't mean we're friends. You hardly know me! I mean, what's my last name?"

"Trusedale."

"Oh. *Oh*," she said again, the second time softer than the first. "You *were* paying attention." Her face came over all sweet, with a good dose of canny, and Sean wished he'd kept his trap shut.

Just then, a bunch of well-dressed young Florentine men burst from the entrance to Enzo's bistro. Laughing, jostling. One of them bumped Aubrey as they passed.

A couple of the men turned to apologise. When they saw who they were apologising to—a long-legged beauty in short shorts, with glowing skin, huge smiling eyes, who was lapping up every ounce of attention—they moved in. All apologies, promises, playing up their accents for the pretty tourist.

Her backpack slid from her shoulder, the lip opening wide. And before he even felt himself move, Sean stepped close, and reached out for the handle; his finger tracing her shoulder, skin warmed by the sun, as he slid it down her arm and into his hand.

He moved in front of Aubrey as he yanked the cord tight, and turned to the men. *"Vai avanti,"* he said. *"Vamoose."*

The young men bowed, held up hands in supplication, one stopped to pat Elwood, who panted blissfully, his tail wagging once in the heat, and off they went.

When Sean turned back Aubrey's eyebrows were halfway up her forehead. Her lips clamped between her teeth as she waited for an explanation.

The fact was, he didn't have one. Not one he cared to verbalise.

So he went with, "Maybe a chaperone is exactly what you need."

"Ha! Sexist much."

"My observations," he said, "have nothing to do with your being a woman and everything to do with the fact you can't keep your damn bag closed."

She held out a finger and he draped the loop of her backpack over the digit. When his finger grazed hers, the lightest imaginable touch, he felt a crackle of electricity.

She gave the cord an extra tug, as if he'd been about to rifle through the thing. But her smile... She liked him. She liked the tension strung between them. That much was crystal clear.

He'd be lying if he said he didn't feel the pull, a leaning towards her effervescence, but, while she was so full of light it was hard not to squint, he'd been burned hollow a long time ago.

"*Gian! Caro amico!* Did those young men bother your friend?"

Sean looked up to find Enzo descending, eyes locked onto Aubrey—his conduit to a conversation outside food, or whether or not it looked like rain.

"Not at all," said Aubrey. "They were hilarious."

"Ah. *Bene. Bene.* That is good."

Knowing the older man would burst if he was not at least given an introduction, Sean said, "Enzo, this is Aubrey, my—"

"Your friend! *Sì.* It is so nice to see you with a friend. And a lovely friend at that!"

Not a friend. Barely an acquaintance. Absolutely a thorn in his side.

In the end, Sean corrected with, "She's a fellow Australian. Aubrey Trusedale, this is Enzo Frenetti. The owner of the fine bistro you see across the way."

"Oh, how brilliant," Aubrey said, reaching out to shake Enzo's hand. "Cannot wait to eat there!"

"So, you and Gian are *not* friends?" Enzo queried, expression near comical in its confusion as he took in the gap between Sean and Aubrey. Or lack of gap more like, as Aubrey had leaned into him until the barest sliver of daylight peeked through.

Sean inched away. One hand curling Elwood's leash tighter, the other shoved into the pocket of his jeans.

"That's right," Aubrey said, grinning. "We are most definitely *not* friends."

"Then… Are you here to check out Gian's wares?" asked Enzo.

"His wares, you say?" Her big Bambi eyes turning his way before glancing down to his shoes then back to his face. Not even trying to hide the fact she'd just checked him out. "Sure. Why not?"

Sean cocked his head. *Really?*

She shrugged. The tiniest movement of her shoulders. *So sue me.*

"Si," said Enzo, chest puffed out, missing the subtleties entirely. "This young man is one of the

most talented artisans I have had the pleasure to meet in my entire life." Was that a tear brimming in Enzo's eye? "He is a marvel. A visionary. Florence is lucky to have him as our adopted son."

"Visionary, you say?" Aubrey was no longer trying to hold back her grin. It was pure sunshine. Utter delight. "Do tell."

"Another time," said Sean, before the two of them steamrollered him with their combined enthusiasms. And he'd already engaged in more conversation than he usually did in an entire day.

Enzo took the hint. "Another time. Till then, I shall leave you young people to your adventures."

With a bow of his head he backed away, banging into Roberto, who was hovering behind him. Enzo flapped his hands at Roberto, chastising him in *presto* Italian as they scuttled off to their respective shopfronts and began beckoning passersby as if nothing had gone on.

The sounds of the crowd bustling around them crept back in as Aubrey turned his way. She took in the dog now leaning against his leg, and the lead gripped in his palm. "So, we are walking, yes?"

Sean baulked. He could just as easily claim work, and head back inside the air-conditioned comfort. Pull out his laptop. Get some admin done. Answer a certain email—

Chances were, she'd follow her feet right inside his showroom and settle in for the day.

"We are walking," he said, regretting the words the minute he said them.

Till her lovely face lit with delight.

"Any place in particular you'd like to go?"

"Every place." She bounced on her toes and clapped her hands and pointed in every direction till he picked one.

"Would you like me to show you my favourite things to do around Florence?"

"Really? That would be grand. I can't imagine why it never occurred to me to ask!"

Sean almost laughed. Or more that he remembered how it felt to do so. "Okay, then. Let's go."

CHAPTER THREE

AUBREY EXPECTED THE delicious Mr Malone to take her some place obvious, like the Pitti Palace or the Uffizi Gallery.

Or some hidden gem of a spot known only to the locals. Some place special to Dante, perhaps. For Sean Malone had a definite sense of a tragic poet about him. All dark hair raked by frustrated fingers, the constantly furrowed brow, the deep voice with that seriously sexy Italian accent as he said things such as *"mi scusi"* and *"grazie"* as they edged their way through summer crowds.

But the man seemed to be wandering, meandering nowhere in particular. Slowly. She tried clicking her fingers at his big beautiful dog in the hopes he'd speed things up. But alas, the velvety grey pup was clearly made for his ambling owner.

Was he trying to shake her off? It was a possibility.

Then again, she *had* tracked him down in the hopes of a little company to slow her down.

Yeah, right, her subconscious perked up, *that's why you tracked the hot man down.*

And yet… More than that, Aubrey was anxious to do the things. To see the places. To experience every experience. To have at the world before…

Before she accidentally pinched herself and awoke from this fairy-tale dream.

Or before something bad happened. And the dream was taken away from her, yet again.

Not that she feared contracting another heart-harming virus. But she could get hit by a Vespa. Bitten by one of the zillion dogs that roamed the city. A piano might fall from the sky and land on her head!

If it happened, it happened. But she would not die knowing she hadn't lived her life with every ounce of joy and fun and heart and purpose and communion she could. She was going to fill her life with wonder if it was the last thing she did.

"You okay?" Sean's voice rumbled into her subconscious.

She came to from her macabre imaginings to find he'd slowed even more, and was looking at her a little askew. "Hmm?"

"You're jumping from foot to foot. Need me to point you in the direction of a rest room?"

"What? Pfft. No! Where I work, I'm the only female in a place with unisex bathrooms. I have the bladder of an ox."

A beat, then, "Do oxen have particularly good bladders?"

"I've no idea. Yes. Probably." She nibbled at her lip, then thought to hell with it. "I know you have this austere aesthetic going on, but if this is

your favourite thing to do in Florence you really
are easily pleased."

His hand played absently with his dog's velvety grey ears; the eerily pale canine eyes looked
at Aubrey in quiet expectation. The human eyes,
on the other hand, those depths of the most stunning blue, watched her in a way that made her
feel jittery. As if she were balanced on the edge
of something. And could fall either way.

"I wasn't aware I had an aesthetic," he said, his
voice like oil over gravel.

"Oh, you totally do. Don't get me wrong, it's
fabulous. All *hands off the merchandise*. Dark
and broody and spare."

Something flashed behind those eyes. Though
she had no idea if it was exasperation or a visual
version of that same crackle and snap she'd felt
when he'd slipped her backpack from her shoulder
earlier. Like static electricity ramped up to eleven.

But then he ran a hand over his jaw and looked
off into the middle distance. Elwood tugged on the
lead and they started ambling once more.

A few steps later, a drip of sweat wriggled
down Aubrey's temple. She drew her tank top
away from her belly and gave it a flap.

She'd always been on the smaller side. Her
brothers joked they'd taken up all the hearty DNA
and she'd got the leftovers. Until she'd fallen sick
and those kinds of jokes had dried up overnight.

Back then, being small had led to her being famously cold at all times. When she was nine, she'd made them all sign a form promising that—when she died falling off the top of the Eiffel Tower or helicoptering over the Grand Canyon—they'd bury her with her socks on.

Now the sweat dripping down her back was just one thing to get used to in her new "normal". As if she had to relearn herself even at a cellular level.

While Sean looked so cool, so crisp, as if he had his own personal air-conditioning unit under his clothes.

Not that there was spare room for such a thing. His polo shirt fitted just right. Snug around impressive biceps, kissing his wide pecs and flat belly every time Elwood yanked on the lead. *Good dog.* His jeans moulded to him as if they never wanted to let go.

"Aren't you hot?" she asked, when she had to wipe sweat out of her eyes.

He looked at her as if he'd forgotten she was even there. *Super. Brilliant plan, Aubs. This is going just beautifully.*

"It's summer. In Florence," was his response.

"Is that a yes? You are hot?"

Say it.

"Yes, I'm hot."

Aubrey held up her hand for a high five. "Gotta love a man with confidence."

The look she received was a killer. Part warning, part glint of humour; as if he *might* finally crack a smile. Would there be dimples? Just one would be more than enough. Two and her ovaries would likely self-destruct.

Not that they were of any use to her otherwise these days.

At that, her heart clenched. Enough for her to wince.

She closed her eyes a moment and shook her head. Trying to shake off the memory of her doctor's face as she'd delivered the news.

No. Not now. Distract! Look at all the pretty Florence. Look at the pretty man!

And so she looked. Distraction the key.

No dimples, but definitely eye creases. Meaning he must know *how* to smile. Unless he was a serial squinter.

Sweat trickled down the side of her face. Her palms burned. Her tongue felt parched. When she took a step the ground didn't quite reach up to meet her.

Dammit.

She hated being forced to say, "I know we've been on a snail's pace, but can we…can we pull up for a bit?"

"You okay?"

Chaperoning her because she'd tricked him into it was one thing. Having him look at her as if she were a delicate flower was quite another.

"You need to promise me something."

A single eyebrow twitched. "What's that?"

"No more asking if I'm okay."

"Right."

"It's a pet peeve." *It really was.* "I'm well aware I look part pixie, but rest assured I'm tougher than I look."

"I have no doubt." His mouth twisted one way, and then the other. "So, coming to me with the request to find someone to carry your bags—"

Hold the phone. Was that sarcasm? She felt the smile start in her belly, a warm hum before it hit her mouth. "Oh, shut up."

He held up both hands in submission.

And she laughed. Actually laughed. For the beautiful broody man had snark.

"Come on," he said, his voice deepening. "We'll stop at the next café."

He held out a hand.

Not for her to hold, she realised, when she went to take it, but to herd her ever forward.

She snapped her hand back into her side. "Sorry. I thought… But, no. I hardly know you! So *that* would be totally weird."

He gave her one more look, measured, reckoning, as if he was not blinded by her sense of humour. As if he was, in fact, figuring her out far too quickly for comfort. Then he walked on.

And Aubrey followed. Her next breath out was a little shaky, and it had little to do with the heat. It was those eyes. Stunners, both. Beautiful even. A deep, mesmerising cerulean blue.

No, Le Mans Blue.

Pearlescent Le Mans Blue, no less.

Le Mans was an absolute classic colour when it came to vintage car paint. Favoured by sixties Chevy owners. Camaros and Corvettes. Elegant and timeless and sexy, it was a favourite for custom paint jobs at her family's auto shop.

And pearlescent paint? Containing mica, a kind of powered crystal that reflected and refracted light, it created sparkle and shimmer, splitting into myriad rich colours depending on where you stood. It was her absolute favourite paint to work with, but super high-maintenance.

She risked a long glance. Took in his preppy hair, his short neat fingernails, the stubborn set to his chin. Yep. High maintenance for sure.

Used to being the boss man. To getting his way. Add deliberate. Not fanciful at all. And she was certain he'd be a right handful.

Why he'd agreed to let her follow him around she had no idea.

She could daydream it was because he'd developed an instant mad crush on her. Something along the lines of the floofy feeling she got every time he looked her way.

Wouldn't *that* be fabulous? A Florentine Fling. Sounded like a cocktail. Or an Agatha Christine novel.

Following through would mean more time in doors, for one thing. Less hours spent walking the streets. Less time out in the heat of the day. Her mother would be delighted.

Laughter curdled in her belly at the thought of video-chatting with her folks. *Hey, Mum! Dad! Meet Sean. He's kept me strapped to my hotel bed for the last week!*

Yeah—no. The occasional Proof of Life pic sent to their group chat of her smiling in front of some fabulous monument was more than enough. They needed the break from worrying about her as much as she needed her independence. Whether any of them were truly ready for it or not.

Pressure suddenly building behind her ribs, Aubrey stopped. Checked in with herself as she'd been taught. Hand over her heart, eyes closed.

Her heart was holding up fine. It was her head that needed sorting out.

She sat on what looked like a plinth meant to hold a pot plant. It could have been a thousand years old. She unhooked her backpack from her shoulder and let it slump to the cobbled ground beside her feet. "Where are we going, exactly?"

Sean's gaze remained glued to her bag—as if it might be about to sprout a head—as he said, "Some place simple. If you're looking for tourist traps, I can take you back to where we started. You'll find some of the best leather and textiles in the city."

"Nah. I'm not a 'stuff' kind of girl. Experiences. Textures. Tastes. Beauty. Art. Inspiration. Feelings—"

The more Sean's face didn't change, the deeper she went.

"I'm here to drench myself in intangibles till they are absorbed into my very skin. Add in the occasional nap, coffee, and time to sketch and I'm golden."

By the end of her rant she was sure she spotted a flicker in those dashing blue depths. Some small measure of recognition at her mission statement. Or maybe he had a dog hair in his eye.

He did the whole looking-off-into-the-distance thing one more time—his hard jaw clenching, his nostrils flaring—then he seemed to come to some sort of conclusion. "Okay, then. Without in any way implying that you're not one hundred per cent okay, if you can carry on another minute I can promise you all of the above. Then coffee."

Aubrey hauled herself to her feet, ignored the way her brain seemed to take an extra beat to catch up, and said, "Done."

He held out an elbow.

"Is that for me to take?" she asked. "After the hand-holding debacle I just want to make sure this time."

This time she got a twitch of his lips for her efforts. At this rate, she'd crack a smile from him in no time.

"Are you always so forthright?" he asked, the oil over gravel back in his voice.

"I'm a Leo," she said. "Your elbow?"

Sean reached out, took her hand and slipped it into the nook.

It fitted there like a glove. As if it had been made to live in that exact groove. Or maybe that was wishful thinking, because he was *so* nice to hold. Built like an championship diver who smelled like cinnamon and wood shavings. Big too. Big enough she felt as if, under his shelter, she could poke her tongue out at any passers-by and they'd not do a thing.

Not that she would poke out her tongue. She was a grown woman living in the twenty-first century.

Because of that she could take on the world, all on her own, just fine.

So why aren't you? her subconscious chimed in.

Because while she'd spent the past two years vibrating with the need to reassert her independence, she also didn't want to do *anything* that might cut her trip short and send her home too soon. Before she had had some idea of what that life back home might look like now that all her original dreams were no longer hers to dream.

If a handsome Aussie wood-wrangler was the fulcrum between both those needs, then so be it.

"So, I'm trying to think how I might repay you for your kindness. I'd offer to show you around

Sydney whenever I get back there, but that's a tad moot, considering your accent. Where in Australia are you from?"

A muscle jerked in his cheek. His jaw clamped so tight he could be mistaken for sudden onset rigor mortis. "Melbourne."

"I'm sorry."

He lifted his voice. "I said, Melbourne."

"No, I heard you. I'm just sorry."

That made an impact. His face registered actual surprise. Maybe even a little amusement! Aubrey actually loved Melbourne. What she didn't like was feeling as if she were banging her head against a wall.

"So, that's how it's going to be?" he asked, his voice dropping. The deep tang of it creating goosebumps all over her arms.

She nodded. "Sydney is the pre-eminent Australian city. Better weather. More landmarks. And the Harbour. I mean, that's where I drop my mike."

"Pick it up. There's not a city in the world that beats Melbourne for the mix of culture, sport, food, architecture, design—"

"Then why are you here?"

A shadow descended, as if a dragon had flown low overhead. Before he had the chance to lean into it, she changed the subject. Closing her eyes tight, she begged, "Please tell me the one thing you want to show me before we find coffee is a copious amount of pizza—"

Sean pulled to a stop. "Open your eyes, da Vinci."

So she did.

To find they had stopped at the end of a cobbled lane. The small thoroughfare opened up to the edge of a huge market. Foods, textiles, trinkets. Hustle and bustle. Noise and energy and commerce.

But she saw all that out of the corner of her eye as Sean had propped her in front of a column at the corner of the square in which a three-foot-high sculpture of a man—biblical, in a loin cloth—resided. Carved into a squared-out alcove in the stone.

Come at it from any other direction and you'd miss it.

And it was glorious. It was everything she had asked for. The movement, the execution, the torment in the twist of his body, the agony of his face.

She took a step closer, her hand sliding out of the protection of Sean's arm. Blackened in the creases, nose and toes worn away, it must have been there for centuries.

"Touch it," said Sean. "I know you want to."

Aubrey laughed. Then laughed some more. "Saucy."

Sean smiled. For a split second. No teeth, but

eye creases galore, and, oh, my God, a dimple. Just the one. And it was perfect.

As if he hadn't seen it coming, as if he would have stopped it if he had, Sean pulled himself together. But not before a seriously adorable flush grazed his cheeks.

"Don't get distracted," he grumbled. "You wanted to absorb, so absorb."

Aubrey was absorbing, only the statue was not her subject. She could happily have been distracted by Sean Malone's face all day long. To say he was sketchable was an understatement. Those cheekbones. The depths of his eyes.

When he tilted his head, his eyes widening, his expression increasingly exasperated, she flapped a hand at him. "Fine…fine." And turned back to the statue.

No velvet ropes here. No signs telling her what she wasn't allowed to do. She moved in, reached up and placed a hand over the statue's foot.

Closing her eyes, she committed to memory the cool of the stone. The mix of rough and smooth. The bumps where the chisel had slipped. The chips that time, and weather, and human interaction had worn away.

It could have been seconds or minutes later when she lifted her hand and opened her eyes.

Around them people milled. Talked. Haggled. Ate. Bought bags, belts, single red roses, soaps in the shape of the pope.

She felt Sean move up beside her.

"That," she said, her voice more than a little rough, "was pure magic. Thank you."

"You're welcome." A beat went by before he added, "I make wood furniture. Chairs, tables."

"I know," Aubrey said. "I cyber stalked you, remember?"

"So you did," he drawled, his voice a rough burr. "I endeavour to make pieces that are both beautiful and comfortable. Solid, artfully crafted, using old, trusted techniques. Pieces that will last. But they have nothing on the carvings you'll find scattered in such inauspicious places all over this city. Picture frames leaning outside shops. Frescos tucked into sconces in the walls. The durability is astounding. The accessibility astonishes. Exquisiteness is so interwoven into this place it's easy to miss it. So I made it my mission to see it."

It was more words than she'd have thought he had in him. And she knew she'd never forget a one.

"Pizza?" he said, and all she could do was nod.

Aubrey held the door open for the little old man with the walking stick she'd befriended while looking over the menu outside the pizzeria.

"Grazie," he said.

"Prego," she returned, holding the door a little longer when her waiter appeared holding her

pizza. Well, hers and Sean's, but she'd have no compunction fighting for the last piece.

She followed the pizza with her nose, taking in the thick airy crust. The sauce a gorgeous oily red, big juicy basil leaves scattered atop. It was so fresh out of the pizza oven, the mozzarella still bubbled.

When she sat Sean held up the pizza cutter, his eyes asking if she was all right with him making the cut. She nodded, too busy holding back the drool till he passed her a slice.

Holding it in two hands, she bit down. "Oh, my God," she managed through a mouthful of crispy slippery goodness, "this is so good."

They didn't speak again, not till the pizza was nothing but crumbs and they were both sitting back, hands on bellies, enjoying espressos.

Elwood—curled up in a ball at Aubrey's feet—made a loud harumph.

"One thing I've noticed in my day and a half here," said Aubrey, "is the number of dogs."

"Late twenties, the Florentine government made it legal for dogs to accompany their owner pretty much everywhere. Only place they're not allowed is the Teatro del Maggio Musicale—the Florence Opera House."

"Hope Elwood's not a big fan of Puccini."

"All good. He's more a metal fan."

Aubrey grinned. Sean frowned, as if disappointed in himself for having made a joke. And her heart kerplunked dramatically inside her chest cavity.

She mentally told her heart to pull its head in.

The man sitting across from her—supremely gorgeous and broody and self-aware as he was—was not to be her test case.

He was Australian. He was here. He actively tried to help her keep her bag closed, meaning he was not about to rob her. He was nice to look at. They were the reasons she'd roped him in to help her out.

She had no intention of letting her crush get away from her.

Her heart was…untried in its current state. It had been through the wringer the past couple of years. The virus had brought about a barrage of damage. It had stopped more than once. It had been on a pacemaker. And she still took meds to keep her arteries nice and open.

Even if she told her family she was good as gold, even while her doctors had signed off on her trip, no one could tell her how much longer it would take to heal, if at all.

Meaning she had to check in, to listen to her body, to trust her instincts. Her instincts said, when it came to Sean Malone, she had to be hands off.

Which shouldn't be a problem as he clearly had no clue what to do with her.

Sure, there was *something* there. For both of

them. A lovely kind of sizzle, purring away deep below the surface. So long as they both refused to act on it, the friction would keep things kinetic. Unstable. No chance they'd be on the same beat, the same breath, and their nascent friendship— yes, *friendship*—could simply kick on.

"You done?" asked Sean.

See. To the point. No room for misunderstandings. She liked that.

"Yes, Malone. I am most certainly done."

Sean wiped the napkin across his mouth. Aubrey didn't stare at his lips as they curved up at the edges. Or the moons that creased his cheeks, more evidence he did, in fact, know how to smile.

Nope. She stood and grabbed her backpack and definitely didn't stare.

As he pressed back his chair, and uncurled his big frame to standing, Sean's forehead creased into perfect horizontal lines as he gave her a look. "What?"

"What, what?"

"I can feel you thinking. Why do I feel like I need to brace myself?"

"What? No! I was just thinking how we are, in fact, most definitely, friends."

Something flashed, dark and mysterious, behind his deep blue eyes. "Friends."

"Yep. We're beyond acquaintances, certainly. Elwood took care of that when he sniffed me in the you know what."

Elwood gave her a look, his tongue lolling lazily out of the side of his mouth. She rubbed him behind the ears. Good boy. An ally after all.

With a wave towards the guys behind the pizza counter as he ushered her around the tables and out into the street, Sean said, "I've seen the way you make friends, picking them up like found pennies everywhere you go."

"I do not. I'm very discerning."

She was! She *got along* with most anyone. She loved hearing people's stories. It had been her way of living vicarious adventures when she'd not been able to afford her own.

But friends? With three big brothers, and working in the automotive industry, most of her acquaintances were male. In fact, nowadays, especially since she'd spent so much time in recovery, Daisy and Jessica were pretty much it when it came to friends she'd class as truly close. Did it help that one split her time between Canada and New York, while the other was British and constantly on tour? What did it say about her if it did?

"Right," said Sean. "The security guard at the museum yesterday."

"Well, I mean, he looked awfully bored. It was only right to try to add a little sparkle to his day."

"The South African couple yesterday. And the waiter. The little old man you helped through the door just before we ate. What do you know about him?"

Aubrey pressed her lips together. "Fine. He's ninety-six, single and has never left Florence. Not once! I'm interested in people. In their stories. In what we, as global citizens, have in common. Aren't you?"

If she could also use her time here to survey as many people as possible in order to find out what made them happy, as she set about figuring out her new normal for when she went back to real life, then so be it!

She felt a small tug, as Sean's hand gripped her backpack, stopping her from stepping out as a family of cyclists zoomed past the pizzeria. She stumbled till her back met his front. A wall of warmth. Of strength. Of Sean.

"Not really. No," he said, his voice close. Close enough a wash of warm air brushed the back of her neck. "I can happily go days without seeing a single person. Just me and Elwood, good coffee and a roof over our heads. That's my bliss."

Aubrey shot him a look over her shoulder to find he was even closer than she'd imagined. Close enough to see the streaks of chestnut in his dark hair. The unreal clarity of his eyes. The way his Adam's apple bobbed when he swallowed.

"I admit the don't-feed-the-bear vibe is a huge part of your appeal," she said, her voice gravelly and not even close to friendly. "And yet… Why do I not believe you?"

Sean's gaze travelled slowly over her face. The touch of his eyes set off spot fires in the strangest places: behind her ears, the backs of her knees, under the balls of her feet. When his eyes once again met hers, the pupils were inky black.

His voice was a burr, scraping against her insides, as he said, "You don't know me, Aubrey. What you choose to believe, or not believe, doesn't affect that. If that fits within the bounds of what you consider a friend, then sure, we're friends."

Knocked a little off her game by the veracity in his eyes, Aubrey rolled her shoulder and Sean let her backpack go.

She moved out into the sunshine. Into the waft and sway of tourists and locals mixing and mingling in the square.

She tried to soak up that energy; that melting pot of joy, of vitality, of life was her bliss. But instead she found herself in a tunnel. Every part of her focussed on the quixotic man, the beautiful puzzle, behind her.

She turned to face him, right as he reached out, his finger sliding beneath the strap of her backpack, lifting it to untwist it and lay it flat. His fingernail scraping over her shoulder as he pulled away.

It was an intimate move, over the hill and far away from merely friendly. In fact, if he was a fraction less the determined isolationist, the deliberate pushing of her buttons when it came to her choice of bag would have felt a hell of a lot like a dare.

"Happy now?" she asked, keeping her chin high.

"Marginally. Though I'd be happier if you weren't wearing it at all."

"Saucy," she said, and this time the look he shot her was less surprised. More cautionary. A warning that she was playing with fire.

Thing was, Leos loved fire.

Maybe Sean was right about one thing. Maybe they weren't friends. Maybe friendship *was* a little too simplistic for their unique and nimble dynamic.

Maybe they were flint and stone. A spark in the night.

Maybe a Florentine Fling wasn't such a silly idea.

A one-night stand. Maybe three. Plenty to see in Florence, and she wasn't in any real rush to move on imminently. She had bottomless funds, enough to keep travelling till the end of time if that was her desire.

And it had been a while since she'd…you know. Before she fell sick, as a matter of fact. No wonder she was feeling so frisky. Out in the world, having handsome Sean fall into her lap.

Surely it would be like riding a bike. So to speak. A big bold way to shed the old her and step into the new. Physically. Mentally. No need for her healing heart to come into it at all.

Sean's phone rang with the famously moody opening strains of "Nessun Dorma". Elwood might like metal, but Sean was an opera man. *Seriously. Could he be any cuter?*

He excused himself before checking the caller ID and answering with a brisk, "What's up?" Then his face came over all frowny; the horizontal lines in his forehead deepening. "Right. No. Of course. I'm on my way." After which he hung up.

For all his lone-wolf, Elwood-and-me-against-the-world vibe, turned out he had people after all.

Though when he stared at his phone, the background was black, bar a clock. No social apps. No goofy picture. Hers had a photo of her and all her nieces and nephews. What looked like a dozen of them in various stages of panic, tears or tantrum as her family tried to get them all in one shot.

She felt a pang at their distance, the little ones in her life. Scrumptious little bundles that they were. And now that the chances of her having her own family were dust, her role as Auntie Aubrey was an even bigger deal. But she wasn't much use to them until she felt useful to herself.

Travel. Experience. Knowledge. Information. The space to build herself some new foundations. To push outside her comfort zone, as it was no longer a place she belonged.

"Malone?" she said, thinking *friends, not flings*. She'd never had a friend she also had a little crush on. But this adventure was all about new experiences, right?

"Sorry," he said, running a hand through his hair. "I have to cut our tour short."

"Problem?"

"Work. I have to go to work. I have my car today, parked in a garage near the shop. I'll drop you back at your hotel on the way."

"Cool. Except you work for yourself though, right? I mean, you're the big boss."

He shot her a look.

"So no one would have a problem if you brought a *friend* along."

He opened his mouth. Shut it. He was a man of few words, but still she quite liked that she'd rendered him speechless.

"Excellent," she said, rocking up onto her toes. "I get to see what the great and wondrous Sean Malone does when he's not playing tour guide. Besides, I'm excellent in a crisis. I might even be of use."

CHAPTER FOUR

SEAN'S CAR WAS GORGEOUS. Her brothers would hate it.

Too pretty. Too European. If they found out she was hanging out with a guy with a Maserati—aka not a Ford—they'd never let her live it down.

Aubrey, who considered herself more open-minded, took a three-hundred-and-sixty-degree tour of the late-model sedan. Metallic black paint. No custom flash. Big shock.

She leant over to peer through the tinted windows to the red leather interior, racing car seats, the big soft rug on the back seat covered in grey dog hair, before standing upright to find Sean watching her over the top of the roof, his keys swinging on the end of a finger.

"Something wrong?" he asked.

"Nope. It's clean-cut. Sophisticated. With just a hint of grunt. It's you."

His eyes narrowed. She wondered which part he had a problem with.

Before she figured out that part was her, she pulled open the door and slid inside. Sean opened the back door for Elwood, who bounded in and licked Aubrey right up the front of her face the moment he saw his chance.

By the time Sean slid into the driver's seat she was spluttering and coughing.

"You—?" He stopped himself right in time.

"Am I what?"

"Can't say. You told me not to."

Aubrey grabbed the edge of her shirt and lifted it to wipe the spit from her tongue. "Seriously? Don't you think that was an occasion that warranted it?"

"You tell me."

Aubrey peeked over the top of her shirt hem to find Sean looking...strangled.

"Can you put your shirt down, please?" he gritted out.

"Why?"

"Because... I can see you."

Aubrey had a gander. Her shorts were high-waisted so there was a smidge of skin showing above her belly button and below her bra. Far less flesh than the world would see if she was wearing a bikini.

She glanced up at Sean and scoffed. Only to find him now gripping the steering wheel and looking out of the front window as if his life depended on it.

Meaning he was trying even harder to keep the sizzle between them locked down than she was.

She cared less about the why than she did about the *oh, my.*

Sean Malone was keen on her. Super-keen.

Friend? Fling? Maybe it was best to not put a label on it and just enjoy.

She slowly let her shirt fall back over her belly, and turned a little on the seat. Her voice dropping a smidge. They were in a small confined space, after all. "I know you're this super-straight, up-standing guy who goes around rescuing women he believes might be damsels in distress, even though they are fierce and strong and perfectly fine thank you very much, but I didn't pin you for a prude."

A muscle twitched in his jaw. His lovely hard jaw. It matched the pulse now beating rather strongly in his throat. When he turned to her, the heat in his eyes was anything but prudish. In fact he looked as if he wanted to ravish her then and there. As if the barest scruple was all that was holding him back.

As if a switch had been flipped and the curtain she'd been standing behind dropped away, all the feels she'd been denying shot to the surface. She wanted it. Wanted him to lean over, slide a hand behind her neck and kiss her. Just the thought of it made her head swim, her palms go clammy and her heart shudder.

It was her heart that stopped things, as it always did. A flicker of panic deep within its damaged depths. Like a big old wall keeping her safe from harm.

Aubrey gave her shirt an extra tug south. "Just in case."

Sean laughed. Except it was really more of a groan. He ran a hand over his mouth before letting it drop to his lap. "If I'd known you would be this much trouble I'd never have piped up at the *galleria*."

"Yeah," she said, leaning back against the cool leather head rest and batting her lashes at him. "You totally would have."

Muttering, mumbling, in Italian no less, the accent doing things to Aubrey's insides that she couldn't hope to contain, Sean faced front, switched on the car, gunned the engine, not once, but twice, before taking off fast enough to press her back into the seat.

Air conditioning flooded the car in glorious cool air in moments but she barely felt it, too surprised by the realisation Sean Malone was using his car to prove a point. He wasn't quite as upstanding, cool-headed, or nearly as strait-laced as she'd led herself to believe.

They were out of the city surprisingly soon, Sean's gorgeous car sweeping them up into the hills. The houses got bigger the further they went, the land plots larger and the landscaping more lush.

Sean eventually turned into a long, curving driveway, passing terraces covered in shrubs and scattered in statues, one boasting a crystal-clear infinity pool, ancient stone walls holding them all in place.

At the top stood a large stuccoed villa. It was at least three stories, with wings and pitched rooves, wrought-iron window frames and Venetian glass lamps. It was like something out of a Cary Grant movie.

The car rumbled to a halt right out front.

"We're here?" Aubrey asked, rather redundantly when first Sean then Elwood leapt from the car. "*This* is where you work?"

"This is where I live."

Aubrey moved slowly, taking in the details anew, with wide open eyes. "Melbourne Schmel-bourne," she muttered. "This is bloody fabulous."

Showing a little speed now he was on a mission, Sean hustled her inside.

Forgoing the ostentatious front steps, they made their way through what had probably at one point been a servant's entrance. It led to a rabbit warren of rooms and halls and stairs, with bits added on over the years, till they burst into a huge open-plan room with shiny wood floors, a big modern kitchen and mis matched wooden chairs around a huge round table.

Aubrey gasped. And not just at the sight of the unbelievable coffee machine. Five times the size of the one at her family's garage. Her brothers would salivate if they saw it.

But the view…

Through the floor-to-ceiling windows tossed open to the elements was a vista of lush rolling green hills covered in classic Italian conifers spearing towards a hazy blue sky. And in the distance, a brown smudge with a couple of recognisable buildings peeking out of the top, Florence proper.

"Aubrey," Sean's voice cut into her reverie, "will you be all right if I leave you here a moment?"

"Yes," she breathed. *You can leave me here for the rest of time.* "Absolutely. Give me the chance to get acquainted with your delightful coffee machine."

"I wouldn't touch her; she's temperamental," said a voice with a strong Italian accent that was *not* Sean's.

Aubrey spun to find a foursome of impressively strong, healthy-looking humans heading up the stairs; two young men and two fabulous young women who looked like Wonder Woman's cousins, all of them in work boots and covered in wood dust with face masks dangling around their necks.

"Hey there," said Aubrey, going for friendly only for her voice to come out as a squeak.

The woman in front, the one who'd spoken—hair pulled back in a severe ponytail, dark eyes wary—gave her a knowing smile. *Pitying.*

"Aubrey, this is my staff," said Sean. "Taking a break, I see."

"We saw you driving up," Wonder Woman's cousin said, a curious gaze flickering between her boss and his unexpected guest.

Sean said nothing. Didn't even budge. How interesting. Aubrey had felt a distance between him and the lovely Enzo back in town. She'd figured it came down to the fact not everyone had her incessant determination to connect. But now, even here, with staff who clearly knew one another well by the way they lounged about his living-space room, she could feel the divide.

Aubrey stepped forward. "I'm Aubrey. Nice to meet you all."

"Flora," the leader said grudgingly, taking Aubrey's hand and squeezing for all she was worth. "The big redhead is Hans, the skinny one is Ben. The one who looks like me is Angelina."

"We're twins," said the other twin, a winning smile creasing her striking face.

"Yes," said Flora, rolling her eyes. "I believe that was implied. What we really want to know is where you came from."

"Flora," Sean chastised.

"*Che cosa?* What?" Flora said, her face all innocence.

Aubrey turned to find Sean leaning against the bench, arms crossed, gaze flat, lit with warning. Telling Flora to back down.

But Aubrey didn't need defending. She might be a half-head smaller than each of them, and they all looked as if they could bench-press her, but she could take care of herself.

She lifted a hand to the mask dangling around

Flora's neck, added, "Your face mask. Looks like it's good for gas, paint, vapours dust, mould. Is it an FreshAir 2000?"

Flora's mouth opened before she looked over Aubrey's shoulder to Sean. "I… I have no idea. Boss?"

Aubrey felt Sean shift. Felt him amble towards her. Felt him stop less than a metre to her left. Felt him as if he were millimetres away, not feet. All tension and bridled heat.

"It's an FreshAir 3500," he said. And, for the first time since she'd made his acquaintance, Aubrey saw a spark of unchecked curiosity light his eyes. "How on earth do you even know that?"

"We use really similar ones in my family shop. The full face, though. Not the half."

"What kind of shop?" That was Ben. Skinny. British accent. Pale skin blotched with pink.

Focussing on him was easier than on Sean, who remained a warm, dark presence at her side. "My family owns an auto body shop called Prestige Panel and Paint back in Sydney. We pimp vintage cars."

"Serious? That's wicked."

"Totally wicked. My dad's a panel beater. Highly respected, countrywide. Race cars were his thing in his youth. My brothers are the spray painters. I'm the details girl. I do the finicky work. We all have to wear these super-sexy suits, like

Hazmat suits. Full air masks. Paint, metal dust. Safety first!"

Sean's four workers nodded along. Even Flora seemed less full-on, now that Aubrey was one of the Face Mask Gang.

While Sean... Sean was looking at her differently. And she soaked it up like a sponge. Even while he was still steadfastly resisting her charm, she was a moth to his flame. Metal shavings to his magnet. Her woman-who-hadn't-been-in-a-relationship-for-over-two-years to his hot man.

"Details," he repeated, after doing the blinking thing, taking his customary "Sean moment" to absorb. Though with that new glint in his eye she felt as if he'd absorbed enough of her to become saturated. "You mean...flames down the sides? Leopards on the hood?"

She rolled her eyes. "And you a supposed *'visionary',*" she said, trying Enzo's accent on for size, waving Italian-esque hands for good measure.

Flora snorted. Then hid it, by clearing her throat.

Aubrey brought out her phone, opened the auto shop's webpage displaying her work, and held it out to Sean.

He took it, his thumb sliding over hers in the handover. A little more slowly than seemed entirely necessary. Was it accidental? Was it deliberate? Not that she was complaining.

He took his time, scrolling. Looking at her work the same way she'd looked at the statue in the square—with time, and respect.

"This is you?" he eventually asked, brow furrowed, all delicious concentration. "You did all this?"

"Mm hmm."

He turned the phone over. To the stained glass heart on her phone case. "You did this too."

"Sure did. My friend, Daisy, is a musician. She used that pic on a single cover, then had the phone case custom made for me for Christmas a year ago, just before I finally went back to work."

"Back?"

Oops.

"Long story." Not one she had any intention of sharing. She was having far too good a time being Aubrey the Unavoidable, rather than Aubrey the Sick.

She moved in closer. Her shoulder happened to rest against his arm as she slid a finger over the screen till it stopped on her favourites. A photo of her putting the final touches on the petrol tank of a Harley Davison made to look as if it were covered in lace. A Camaro decked out to look as if it were covered in snake skin.

"Let me see," said Flora, finding a way to shuffle between them, forcing Aubrey to take the phone and Sean to let go as he moved away.

After a few long moments Flora turned to

Aubrey, her eyes accusing as she said, "You are very talented."

It was so unexpected Aubrey laughed. "Damn right I am. But thank you."

Flora gave her a nod, mouth downturned. *Respect.* Before reverting to Italian, turning her back and moving in on Sean to say, *"Il capo. Il telefono."*

And Sean's face came over all broody and dark. Like an island in a storm.

Making Aubrey realise how much he'd lightened up over the past few hours. She allowed herself the little glow that came with being pretty sure she had something to do with it.

While Sean and Flora talked in fast, furious yet muted tones, the rest of the crew hovered. Shuffling from foot to foot. Waiting for instruction. Deferential.

Which was when Aubrey realised Flora's vibe wasn't possessive. It was *protective.* Making her wonder why big, strong Sean Malone would need protection. Especially from the likes of her.

"Hey, guys," Aubrey stage-whispered, "I'm going to make myself a coffee. And I'm happy to make more if anyone's keen? Don't mind a little temperamental." She edged towards the fancy coffee machine, wriggling her fingers to encourage the shufflers away from the talkers.

Angelina, Ben and Hans all nodded, following the promise of caffeine. While Sean shot her a grateful smile. Not huge. More a tilting of the lips. A warmth around the eyes.

Still she might have stumbled just a little at the sight of it. Actually stumbled. As if she'd tripped over non-existent shoelaces.

He knew it too. The smile deepened. A sudden flash of teeth, a crinkle around the eyes before he turned back to Flora, who was looking at him as if he'd grown an extra head.

Aubrey bit her lip to stop from grinning like a loon. Then set to searching through what turned out to be some well-stocked cupboards to make the team a bunch of very fine cups of coffee.

All the while realising that Sean Malone was perfectly aware of how he affected her. And he let her stick around anyway.

"Aubrey," said Sean as he ambled up to her spot leaning against the kitchen bench where she had plonked herself a good hour earlier, taking the time to send pictures to family and friends when the others had all moseyed downstairs.

Fine, so she might have explored first, away from all the loud banging and whirring coming from the workshop, nosing around the place to find a lot of locked doors. And even more traces of elegantly shabby unfurnished space. As if Sean lived out of only two or three rooms like some kind of mythical prince, trapped in his castle.

Though from what she could discern it was self-inflicted. His refusal to settle in, to open up, a choice.

Did people really just accept that? Or was she that much more bullish when it came to making herself seen—the product of being the youngest with three loud big brothers? If so, she was glad of it. He was worth the effort.

"Hey," she said.

He moved to lean against the bench beside her. Not too close. But not too far either. "Sorry that took so long."

"Hey, you came here to deal with whatever that was. I'm just a stowaway."

Sean gave her a look. Considering, measuring; little sign of the wall he usually held in place. Because he was home? Or because of the series of infinitesimal shifts in their dynamic that had happened since?

"Tomorrow," Sean said, leaning in a little; his voice deep, soft, intimate.

"Tomorrow?" she parroted back, her voice more than a little rough.

"I'll make up for it."

"Oh. Okay." Not one to look a gift horse in the mouth… "How? I need details."

"I'll take you places. Touristy places. Places Machiavelli once stood. Michelangelo. Galileo. Places you can stop, and sit, and sketch. Or try to touch works of art when the guards aren't looking.

Places so rich with history and touristy splendour you'll forget the David's name."

Aubrey gasped. "Never! He's it for me. My one and only. Once I figure out how to help him down off his perch, the two of us are outta here."

"Nevertheless."

Aubrey nudged her chin towards the stairs. "Are you sure? Your crew looked plenty filthy. And I heard noises. Clearly there's some actual hard work going on…somewhere within the walls of this crumbling palace of yours."

The edge of Sean's mouth tilted. "It's no palace, believe me."

"A little big for one guy, perhaps?" she said, not exactly pressing for personal info about his relationship situation, yet totally pressing.

"Mmm. It was the huge wine cellar that sold it," he said, rubbing a hand over the dark grit that now shadowed his chin. "Since the place is built into the side of the hill, the basement has exterior access—two big old wooden doors lead right onto the driveway, which is perfect for pickups and deliveries so I had the cellar converted into a workshop."

"Sacrilege," she whispered.

"I think you mean ingenious."

And once again, she saw a flash of teeth as he smiled. She'd wished it, but now she wasn't sure she could handle it.

She looked away so that she could control the

air in and out of her lungs. "You don't have to. To-morrow. This afternoon has actually been exactly what I needed. A rest day. Just focus on whatever it was that brought you zooming back here in your fancy car, okay?"

He ran a hand through his hair. Giving it a hard tug at the end. It was telling. A sign things were not totally cool in Sean World. "It was nothing."

"Nothing. Okay. If you say so."

He gave her that look. The one that warned her not to push.

But the thing was, she was a Leo, the young-est of four, and the only girl; pushing was the only way she knew to get things done. "If you're determined to keep spending time with me, you will tell me eventually. You know that, right? I'll niggle till you spill. It's a big part of my charm."

Sean's hand dropped to the bench, his little finger curling over the edge a hair's breadth from her own. The look he gave her was hooded. Sexy lines furrowing his brow. Lips tilted at the edges.

Nobody should look the way he looked when he was trying not to look like anything. It really wasn't fair to the rest of the human race.

Then a shadow passed over Sean's eyes before he dragged his gaze away to look out of the big picture windows, to the sky beyond. She thought that might be it. Conversation closed.

Till he said, "We—in this space—work on

commissions. Creating, from concept to completion, everything from a single nursery chair for a royal baby, to a boardroom table that had to be sent by ship, then hauled to the thirtieth floor of a skyscraper in Qatar by way of a crane. The Malone Mark on a piece carries weight."

Not an ounce of apology for his success. She loved it.

She leant her chin on steepled fingers and begged, "Tell me more."

A cough of laughter. His shoulders relaxing a smidge lower. The furrows in his brow easing. It was quite lovely to watch him unwind. To know he felt comfortable enough to be that way with her.

Then he said, "If you keep your trap shut longer than half a second I will."

Aubrey mimed buttoning her lips, even while her heart thudded at the sudden flash of authority coming her way.

Sean's gaze dropped to her mouth. Where it stayed. Lingered. His chest rising and falling. His jaw tightening.

And any *comfort* she might have felt disappeared as fast as a drop of rain on a hot car roof.

She might have made a sound. A squeak. A moan. Enough that Sean breathed out hard and lifted his eyes to hers. If he didn't see spades of lust therein he wasn't looking hard enough. And from where she stood he was looking. Hard.

"The Malone Mark?" she said, her voice scratchy against the tight confines of her throat.

"Right," he said. She wondered if he knew he'd had to physically shake himself back into the conversation. "I received an email yesterday morning. A commission request. I'd yet to respond as I'd yet to decide if it was something I could do. The...person making the enquiry followed up. Phoning here. From a private number. Flora took the call as the only person who ever calls the landline is her dad."

"If it's a private number how did this...commissioner get it?" she asked, but only after unbuttoning her lips. And once more it caught Sean's gaze.

This time when he looked away he ran a hand over his face. "He's an old friend of the family. Only person who'd have given him the number is my father."

"Right," said Aubrey, even though she didn't understand at all.

Sean's voice was solemn. Sombre. The word *father* dropped like a lead balloon.

She got that family could be a code word for chaos. How fraught those connections could be. How fragile and how fierce. Her own family was mad. But she loved them so much. Enough that they were absolutely her Achilles heel.

They were all in, each and every one. From her mum and dad, to her brothers, their wives, their gorgeous growing broods of kids.

The fact that she loved her family so ferociously was half the reason she'd taken Viv's gift.

While Viv's only proviso was that she begin in Florence, Aubrey's only proviso was that before she spent a cent on her trip, she'd pay her parents back every cent they'd lost in taking care of her when she was ill.

It had been a big ask. But Viv had been adamant that her gift was giving her more joy than she could explain—and that she had billions to spare and no one to pass them on to bar Max, her dog.

It had served as a wonderful distraction. Showing her parents their flush bank account, then scooting out of the door and into the cab waiting to take her to the airport.

All that in mind, Aubrey treaded carefully, keeping her voice light as she asked, "Is his being friends with your family a good thing? Or no?"

"It's…complicated."

"Of course it is."

"Are you mocking me?" he asked, shooting her a hot dark look that made her knees give out. Just a bit.

"Constantly!" she shot back.

Sean laughed that time. Really laughed. A rough rolling release of energy that barrelled through him till he had to bend over, hands on knees, to breathe.

"You okay down there?" Aubrey asked, her voice just for him.

He stood and she stood with him, eyes locked. Leaving Aubrey feeling a little light in the head. She could have put it down to those baby-blue stunners, but her low blood pressure was another thing she had to manage nowadays. And it had been a while since she'd eaten.

She leant back against the bench to regain a semblance of balance. Covering the slow return of blood to her head with fast talk. "By the intense back and forth earlier, I'm thinking Flora wants you to take the gig."

"It's not her call."

"Of course, Mr Boss Man Malone decides where the Malone Mark goes. But it's clear she cares about the business." And the crew. And him. Even though even now Sean stubbornly refused to give. "What's her take?"

"It's good exposure."

"And you don't want to take it because…"

"Family. Complicated. I thought I'd made that clear."

Definite hot button. "Flora is close with her family?"

"Flora and Angelina are Enzo's daughters."

"Enzo? From the *bistro*?" Enzo who Sean acted as if he barely knew? Jeez, talk about complicated.

"His wife died not long after I arrived. I heard him tell the others in the street that the girls were at a loss. Flora especially. She refused to step up, to take her mother's place in the bistro, which broke his heart anew. While Angelina broke more plates than she served and he didn't know what to do with her. I'd met them both once or twice. Knew they were capable. So I offered them work."

It might well have been the first time in Aubrey's life that she'd been rendered truly speechless.

She stood there, facing him now, and took him in. This man. This walking dichotomy. This fascinating complicated creature she could not resist doing everything in her power to unravel. Because she could sense, at his core, he was something truly special.

"It seems you have quite the collection of damsels in distress."

"Try telling Flora that."

"Yeah, no."

He laughed again, but this time it was contained. Measured. He had himself back under control. Pity.

While Aubrey felt as if the foundations beneath her feet weren't quite as steady as they had been a few moments before.

She'd thought she had him figured out. Big, serious, knight-in-shining-armour complex. But in looking after the likes of Flora—in seeing in her a need and filling it—he hadn't done so because he'd thought she was weak. Or broken. Or because he was tight with her father. He'd taken her in because he was there. Because he could. Because it was the right thing to do.

Sean Malone might be deeply sexy, but he was also a very good man.

And Aubrey found herself forced to admit there was more that drew her to him than his ridiculous hotness. Or the urge to mess with his adorable uprightness.

It was the shadows that called to her too. The darkness in those beautiful eyes. It hooked her right through the gut. Whatever was going on with his family had a grip on him. It haunted him. This was a man who'd known loss. And guilt. Two emotions she knew intimately.

"Seems it's been a tense couple of days," she managed.

"I had no idea how tense, till laughing gave me an actual stitch." He lifted a hand to his side. His T-shirt lifted to reveal a quick flash of skin. Muscle. One side of a ridiculously defined V dipping into his jeans.

Aubrey's mouth went dry. "Can you put your shirt down, please?"

"Hmmm?" He realised after a beat she was throwing his own words back at him. Only this time there was no room for misunderstanding. Or mocking.

He slowly let his shirt drop and when his eyes met hers the heat was real. Matched by her own.

"So," she said, pausing to lick her lips. "I do believe you've been using me these past couple of days, Sean Malone. As a distraction from your real life."

Lines flickered over his nose a moment before his eyes filled with apology. He was far too easy.

"Relax," said Aubrey with a flap of her hand. "I've totally been using you, too. I thought that much was clear."

Then she gave him a punch on the arm. Because…three big brothers. And because—for all her bravado, her ability to talk to strangers, and ask questions, and stand up for herself—her heart… Her damn heart was pounding. And she wasn't ready for it to be tested like this.

She simply didn't trust the busted muscle beating in her chest would hold up under real pressure. And there was too much she wanted to do, wanted to see, wanted to be at peace with in her life, before she put it to that test.

"Coffee?" she asked, moving away from the man, back to the safety of the big machine with its noise and busyness. "I worked in cafés for a while. Coffee art was my thing. Watch this. I have skills."

Sean stepped in closer. Only she knew he wasn't watching the cool, double-layered glass in her hand as she slowly poured the hot frothy milk into a shape. He watched her face. In a way that made her think it was simply a thing he liked to do.

"Before or after the custom-paint-job gig?" he asked. His voice different. More intimate.

"As well as. I'd been saving up the big bucks for a world trip. Got as far as a music festival at the Faelledparken in Copenhagen a couple of years back."

"The Ascot Music Festival."

Coffee art forgotten, Aubrey dropped both glass and jug to the bench. "Yes. How do you even know that?"

"It's how I met Ben. I was heading to the Opera House to see something by Verdi—*La Traviata*—when I stumbled on Ben and the girl he'd been travelling with, right after they'd been robbed. Bags sliced open on the train. They were frantically emptying their bags in search of their tickets to the music festival. It was sold out. No other way in. I offered to shout them tickets to see the Verdi instead. Took them about half a second to accept. Good sports."

"Opera over pop?"

"For me, well, yeah. My mother played nothing but when I grew up. It's…familiar." The shadows were back. His voice a little faraway as he said, "Only one band I can remember wishing I'd seen there. Not the headline act, another one—"

"Dept 135?"

"Ah, yes, actually. One of the band members owns a couple of my chairs, which is pretty cool.

That was the night they first played with Daisy Mulligan, you know?"

It was Aubrey's turn to laugh. "Daisy is one of my absolute best friends."

Sean's disbelief was clear.

"Seriously! She's the one who searched the internet for you. Who turned me into your stalker. Who used that heart picture on my phone on one of her single covers."

"You know Daisy *Mulligan*."

Aubrey pulled out her phone, scanned till she found the picture taken during that same festival, the day the girls had visited Viv in the hospital.

Sean leaned to look over her shoulder. "That's Daisy Mulligan."

"No. Where?"

Sean was too discombobulated to join in the joke. "And that... Is that *Vivian Ascot*?"

Aubrey turned, just a fraction. But enough to find Sean's face devastatingly close to her own. Close enough to count his thousand perfect lashes. To see stubble sprouting all over his perfect jaw.

Aubrey tipped her phone away, and moved, just enough so that her breath no longer mingled with his. "Sure is. And that's it as far as my famous friends go. We all met at the festival and stayed in touch since. It's no 'I make furniture for royalty', but I'll take it."

Sean leant back against the bench, ankles crossed, his arms doing the same. "What do you mean you only got as far as Copenhagen? What happened in Copenhagen?"

Dammit. How had she let herself lead the conversation there again? There she was telling herself it was her mission to loosen him when he kept doing the same to her.

Making her forget. For a while.

When she was with him, it was all about the now. Soaking in his calm. Deciphering his microexpressions. Seeing how far she could push him before he pushed back.

With him, she felt like herself for the first time in a really long time.

"I had to go home," she said when the silence stretched out too long.

"Because?"

"Reasons. Now stop distracting me with your questions. And your shirt flapping. And your handsome face." She went back to her coffee. Heated up the froth again and started over. "There."

She presented him with the glass.

He looked at the "art" as instructed, only to find no palm leaf or heart as they were no doubt wont to do down at his local, but something far more R-rated.

His gaze lifted to hers. Humour, connection, heat.

"Seriously?" he asked, his voice a rumble.

"Told you I have skills."

CHAPTER FIVE

LATER THAT EVENING, after the crew had all insisted on popping their heads upstairs to say goodnight to Aubrey, who had plied them with coffee—and coffee art—all day long, Sean found Aubrey sitting at the small table on the balcony by the lounge, arms wrapped around her knees, feet tucked up on the chair, as she looked out over the city.

The sun was slowly sinking lower in the sky and the gauzy heat of the day was gentled by a cool breeze.

He could have offered her a lift home, at any point. But he hadn't.

He could have insisted, using work as an excuse. But he didn't.

He'd kept her near. Aware that his crew had fed off her quirky energy in a way he'd never seen in the workshop before. They were jovial. Chatty. Including him in their ribbing, which they never did, ever.

He thought of the South African couple at the café in Piazza Della Signoria the day before. The security guard at the Galleria dell'Accademia.

Aubrey had a way of drawing people out. In following Aubrey's lead, his crew had found permission to be themselves.

Which was on him. He knew that. He'd fostered that sense of distance. Of work and no play. He'd not moved to the other side of the world on a whim. It had been a huge risk. A massive undertaking. Yet he'd had no choice but to create a new foundation for his life after his last one had been ripped out from under him.

Sean's eyes drifted closed as his sister, Carly, once again snuck into his subconscious. Memories bobbing up like treasures weighed down below the surface. The kind incessant tides eventually set free.

Only one thing had changed in his landscape to make those weights no longer function as they had. One person causing him to lose that grip.

If he was smart he'd have said, "Big day tomorrow. I'll take you home."

Instead he said, "Hungry?"

She turned, her face relaxed. And so very lovely in the dwindling evening light.

If *she* was smart she'd yawn and say what a lovely day it had been but she needed her beauty sleep. Instead she gave him a long, direct, discerning look, before saying, "Famished. What does the palace cook have in store for us?"

He leant his forearms along the back of the chair beside hers. "Coffee first? Then pasta. I'll make both."

Hands locked behind her head, she watched him from beneath her lashes. "Got anything stronger?"

"I remember seeing a bottle of wine somewhere. Left behind by the last people who owned the place. Might be vintage. Might be vinegar."

"Stronger," she said, her eyes not leaving his.

"What's the thing these days? Aperol Spritz?"

She scrunched up her nose. "Too dry."

"A Bellini? Negroni?"

"Now you're talking. You have the goods?"

"The crew think I haven't noticed the gear they've snuck into my pantry over the years. Serves them right if we clean them out."

Aubrey let her feet drop to the ground, before unwinding herself from the chair. She lifted her arms in a stretch, swaying as if moved by the last breath of the light evening air.

He'd picked up such a strong sense of vulnerability, seeing her sitting on the floor of the gallery, sketching away. Now he saw grace and gall, straightforwardness, doggedness, kindness. There was more vitality, more life, in her little finger than he'd lived in a year.

When she sashayed past him and headed inside she left him feeling restless. As if he were ruled by currents. Stormy winds. Eddying and swirling. Begging for release. Release in her.

But he held back. Years of self-denial had left his willpower strong. Burnished to a sheen.

Moving to the kitchen, looking to the world a normal man, he found what he needed. Poured the gin by eye. Campari. Vermouth. Mixed, then poured into two glasses over ice.

"You've done that before," she said.

"You worked in cafés, in between times. I worked in bars."

"Of course you were a bartender. I've always had a thing for bartenders."

He grabbed a fresh orange one of his guys had no doubt picked from one of the trees in his orchard out back, adding a spritz of zest at the end. He licked a drop from the palm of his thumb, made eye contact, and said, "Because they're good for a chat-up line?"

"Because they're good at making cocktails."

A smile. He felt it start in his throat before it hit his mouth. A tightness and a release. "True. I made my fair share through uni."

"Chat up lines?"

"Cocktails?"

"Ah. You were studying…?"

"Architecture."

"Of course. All the hot, upright guys study architecture."

He'd known this woman a day and a half. years to feel comfortable enough with one In his world—private schools, old money, parents on the board of the Opera Foundation, dinner at the dinner table every night at seven—it took people another to be that honest. If ever.

Ask him and he would have said he preferred those people. Found ease in the aloofness. Yet his truth was that he found every single thing about Aubrey as refreshing as all get out.

"What gave you the idea that I'm upright?" he asked, holding eye contact, his voice a little rough.

"I… Well…" She swallowed. Rendered speechless for a brief moment.

He slid her drink across the counter. Waited till her fingers wrapped around the glass before letting go. "Sit. Drink. I'll have dinner ready in fifteen."

He pulled out the sauce he'd made the night before, and popped it back on the stove. Filled another pan with water, salt and penne.

Then smiled, feeling unusually good about the world, as he watched the water come to the boil.

A half-hour later they sat next to one another at the round table, digesting.

Candlelight flickered over Aubrey's face, creating hollows in her cheeks, picking out flashes of red in her hair. It was romantic as hell. Till Elwood groaned as he rolled over on his bed in the corner.

"So architecture wasn't for you in the end?" Aubrey asked out of the blue.

Sean picked up his drink; a fine local red she'd somehow had delivered to the villa during dinner using an app. "My mother's father was a cabinet maker. He taught me how to hold a chisel before I could hold a pen. After the first couple of years of uni, I…decided the hands-on part of design—

shaping, honing, pushing the envelope—was where I fit best. It made sense to shift."

Aubrey gasped and sat forward, eyes wide and delighted. "You mean you didn't *graduate*. That so doesn't fit with the Sean Malone aesthetic. Why?"

Sean looked into the swirling shadows of his drink.

"Well, that was a longer than normal pause, even for you. Meaning you have no intention of telling me."

He looked up to find her watching him. No accusation in her warm gaze. Just interest. A seeking of truth.

The truth was that that was the time his sister, Carly, was getting into real trouble. His parents, people whose lives were built around how things appeared, let her get to the brink before admitting they'd lost control.

The instant he'd found out, Sean had deferred uni and moved home to help. To reconnect. To talk some sense into his little sister. It seemed to help, too. Carly moved back home. Stopped seeing her boyfriend. Seeing progress, Sean, who'd not been raised to sit on his hands, had leapt at the chance of a side hustle to fill his time. He spent all his time brushing up on his woodwork skills and took up where his grandfather had left off.

First product show he'd entered he'd hit the market with a splash. The success a counterpoint to the desperate quiet of home he'd sought to escape. And he'd lost sight of why he'd come back at all…

The sense of weight back in his belly, Sean shook his head slowly.

Aubrey's smile twisted. "You're deeper than you look, you know."

"You have no idea," he said, hoping she might take heed. Realise how very different they were.

Instead she shivered, as if the thought of hidden depths was delicious.

He'd known she was trouble the second he saw her. A sixth sense warning him of danger. It had never occurred to him *she* was the danger. That he was the one in trouble.

"Fine," she said with a roll of her eyes. "I won't go rummaging around in your shadows, so long as you know that means you also get zero access to mine."

"Your shadows."

"Baby, I have shadows like you wouldn't believe."

Her voice was pure sass. But a flicker behind her eyes told him she wasn't all quips and lip. That there might be something hidden there after all.

He lifted his drink and took a sip. Was he okay with that? With not knowing? When he'd worked so hard to keep his life simple. Disconnected. No deep connections meant no drama. Meant no heartache. No loss.

Aubrey nibbled on her bottom lip and his concerns became muddled. "If I can't ask why you didn't graduate, or why hearing from your father's friend has you in such a tizz, or why you clearly love red wine but had none in the house, then what can we talk about?"

He leaned back. "The weather."

"Great. It's bloody hot, right? Okay, now we've exhausted the weather. How about…? The Malone Mark. I'm going to be indelicate here."

"Big shock."

"I know, right? The pieces you are working on downstairs are seriously lovely, but unless you sell each for tens of thousands, how can you afford this place? Not to mention the car. And that pretty window right in the centre of town."

"The Malone Mark—"

"Carries weight. Yes, you did mention that, in a rare yet refreshing brag."

"I was going to say, is only a small part of my business. The custom pieces are the wow factor. Perfect for Instagram. Creates name recognition. Desire. That trickles down into my wholesale business."

"Right. I get it. Like the way car manufacturers release drool-worthy, futuristic concept cars that make we poor slobs go out and buy their regular street version in the hopes of having a little of that lustre rub off on us. Smart thinking, Malone."

"Exactly."

His family had never understood. Telling

friends about his big commissions but not the fact they probably all plonked their backsides daily onto his wholesale stools in their kitchens. The same way they'd talked up his big accomplishments, over Carly's smaller ones. Not that he'd ever called them up on it. Not in time, anyway.

Sean shook the thought away. Said, "It was all fairly organic really. Once I became focussed. One chair in particular found traction. Became a bit of a thing when it was featured heavily in a popular TV show—"

"Oh, my God. You designed the Iron Throne!"

"What? No. It was used by the hosts of a morning show in the States. My designs are based on form and function. Not fear and pain."

"Right. Sorry. Go on."

Laughing now, relaxing, and rather amazed at both, Sean kept talking. Talking more than he remembered talking in years.

It was all due to her. Her gift was born of genuine interest. But after the "you'll never know my shadows" comment he wondered if it was also a way of not having to reveal much of herself.

"Several manufactures tracked me down after that chair. Offered to buy the design. Never much wanted to work for someone else, so I took a risk. Went into manufacturing it myself. I now have three plants building reproductions back in Australia."

"Hell of a commute."

"No commuting. This is my base now. The operations back home are run by highly competent people. I oversee remotely."

"You *never* go back?"

"I never go back."

She gave him that gaze, the one where all the shimmer stilled. Where she focussed. Every part of her direct. Where he felt like a fly caught in her amber.

"Did you run away from home, Sean?"

"I thought we agreed not to touch on that."

"So that's a yes. And I agreed. You didn't. Tell me about your family."

"Tell me about yours."

"Are we going to do this now?"

Were they? Before he could form a thought, Aubrey leant forward, challenging. Said, "My dad, Phil, is a panel beater."

"Old news."

"You want more? Okay. In his spare time, Dad paints. Abstracts. Wild gorgeous colourful things. He's the one who gave me my love of art. He'd give anything to come here, to see the greats. But he busted his knee a few years back and wouldn't be able to handle the travel. He's so thrilled I'm finally here, that I'm doing this—"

At the last, her voice cracked. Just a little. A hint, perhaps, into the shadows she made him promise not to nudge. Only now he knew they were there, they reshaped his understanding of her. Made her feel less like a flash of light blinking in and out of his existence. And far more real.

"Mum, Judy," she said, pulling herself back together, "is a homemaker. I have three brothers, all older. Have I mentioned that? I tend to, pretty quickly. They do loom large. I'm twenty-six and I'm sure our mum stays up till she hears we're all safe and sound."

Her next breath was deep and shaky, the challenge with which she'd started the conversation having dulled from her eyes. Sean felt a strong need to put a stop to this, whatever it was.

"Aubrey," he said, his voice unexpectedly raw.

But she stilled him with a look. As if she wanted to get this out. *Wanted* him to know. To see her. To understand her. To know that this—whatever it was that was happening between them—wasn't normal for her either.

"So," she went on. "My brothers have produced a zillion children between them, each of whom I could eat up in one gulp, they are that delicious. I miss them all desperately. And have no doubt they miss me as I am the most amazing auntie there ever was."

Something dark flickered in her eyes then. Something so big she swayed with it. Heartache? Sorrow? No, it looked a lot like *defeat*. But, it couldn't be that. He couldn't imagine Aubrey allowing it. She'd look it in the eye and say, not happening.

And while pressing back, asking questions, opening up, letting her in, was miles outside anything he'd done in a while, in years, watching this woman flounder was enough for him to say, "Their names?"

"Hmmm?"

"Your brothers. What are their names?"

A light flickered in the darkness. "Adam. Craig. Matt."

"They good to you? When they loom?"

"Phenomenal. And annoying." The pain in her eyes eased. The light returning. "They could take down the likes of you with their little fingers."

He leant forward. Putting his glass next to hers. So close it clinked. "Left or right?"

A muscle twitched under her eye, and the edge of her sweet mouth curled into a devastating smile. The kind that took a man's legs out from under him. "Take your pick."

"Mmm."

"Now it's your turn."

Sean's next breath burned. Helping her play was one thing, but it wasn't a game to him.

Yet something in her face, the slight tremble still wavering beneath the bravado, fractured something inside him. Shearing away a great chunk of the wall he'd built up inside, like the edge of an iceberg falling into the sea.

"Margot," he said, speaking his mother's name out loud for the first time in nigh on five years. He held eye contact as if Aubrey were a life preserver and he a man who'd suddenly found himself lost at sea. "My mother's name is Margot. She's a lady who lunches. And sits on charity boards. She was an interior designer. A very good one. Inherited my grandfather's eye for shape."

"And your father?" she asked, her voice unusually soft, her gaze rich with empathy. "The one with the friend."

"Brian." Sean felt his head squeeze as he tried to push away the vision of the last time he'd seen his father. Broken, in utter shock, a shell of the man he'd once been; sitting in their big cold house, Carly's wake going on around him while he held tight to a photo of his only daughter when she was just a little girl.

"He was—" Sean stopped, cleared out the frog in his throat "—*is* a financial advisor. Straightlaced. Clear morals. When I decided to throw every cent I had at the chair that made my name, I was sure he'd try to talk me out of it. But he supported it all the way."

"Of course he did," said Aubrey. "If he's anything like you he's both savvy and intrepid. If he saw the light in your eyes when you talk about your work, I'm sure supporting your idea was a cinch. How about siblings? Any brother or sisters who drove you crazy?"

Sean shook his head. He wasn't going further. He wasn't going *there*. In fact he'd gone a mile

his head was swimming. Caught as he was between the urge to put space between himself and this rare creature who deserved far more than the shell of a man he'd become, and the instinctive, survivalist need to soak up whatever life force she could spare.

"You can stay. There is a spare room in use. Staff have crashed here once or twice when a commission neared its end date and they weren't yet done."

"I'm not staff."

"No, you're not. In fact you're the first person I've let in the front door whom I don't pay."

"Hey, whatever gets you through the night."

It took him a moment. "Jeez, Aubrey, I didn't mean—"

"Mocking!" She lifted her head, her big whisky-brown eyes soft with desire. "God, you're easy."

No, he *wasn't*. He was hard, and stubborn, and fractious. He'd created a life in which he gave away little and asked for less. "Aubrey—"

She snuck a finger to his lips. Pressing so he had no choice but to hold his breath.

"Just shut up, okay?" she said, her eyes bright. "Stop trying to get rid of me. You might think you're all that, that you can out-stubborn me, but you have no idea who you are dealing with."

"Neither do you."

Her head tipped to one side, her breath leaving slowly between soft lips, she said, "You knew what you were doing when you 'let' me follow you around today. You knew what you were doing when you 'let' me jump in the car with you. You know what you're doing now. Now prove it."

Her words were big, calling him out in order to elicit a reaction. But he could feel the quiver beneath them. The fear that he might deny her. That she might yet be made to look a fool.

She was feeling this too. The speed of it all. The sense that it was out of their control.

But Sean was *all* about control. It was his anchor. It had saved him when he'd not been certain he deserved to be saved. And he was done letting anything take him places he wasn't ready to go.

So he reeled it in. And held on tight.

He lifted a hand to Aubrey's chin, cradled it, looked from one of her bright beautiful eyes to the other. "Come to bed."

She stilled. "Which bed?"

His thumb ran down the side of her cheek, the feel of her skin—warm and soft and giving—creating whorls of heat inside him. "This is not the time for mocking. Come. To. Bed."

"Are you kidding?" she said. "It's the *perfect* time for mocking. Otherwise you will totally fall in love with me and we can't have that because I'm on holiday so will be gone before you know it. And you'll be stuck here, pining, and—"

Sean quieted her with a kiss.

It was the only way.

It was a soft kiss. No more than a meeting of the lips. Breaths held, eyes open.

Then, with the sweetest moan ever known to man, Aubrey softened. All over. Her hand flattening against his chest, her body melting into his.

The kiss, so sweet, so soft, soon turned into something more. A flood of relief. Of release. Of reckoning.

No more tiptoeing around the escalating attraction that had been brimming between them from the moment they met. It was a tidal wave, no holding back. He bore the full force of her want. Her need.

Her words echoed in his head.

"You knew what you were doing when you 'let' me jump in the car with you. You know what you're doing now. Now prove it."

He lifted her into his arms, shocked to find how little there was of her. Her delicacy hidden by the sheer force of her personality.

Kissing her still, he carried her into his bedroom. His curtains were open, an eerie mix of moonlight and the final breaths of daylight falling over the room.

He kissed her once, then, holding her tight, helped her onto the bed. And followed.

Her hair splayed out near his pillow. Her eyes, dark in the low light, looked up at him.

What he saw there floored him. The sheer honesty of her feelings. Her desire.

Her hand reached up to his face. Her fingers traced his bottom lip. The line of his nose. The curl of his eyebrow. Her thumb returned to his mouth, tracing his top lip this time. Her gaze following.

"I will be compelled to draw you one day," she said, her voice husky, and low. "I'll capture a moment, when you're not expecting it. So you don't pull a face."

"Stalker."

"That I am."

"Just so long as you don't compare me to him."

"Him?"

"The David."

A beat, then, "Who?"

"Atta girl."

When her fingernails scraped up the sandpaper edge of his jaw, he sucked in a breath. Only to see her smile.

"You look so sweet," he rumbled, "but it's all an act."

"I know, right?"

Sean laughed. *Laughed.* Joy flowed through him, freely, unfettered. It had been so long since he'd experienced the emotion, he no longer had the skill to temper it.

He gently brushed her hair away from her face as they drank one another in. Savouring the bittersweet ache of waiting on the brink, when their bodies, their eyes, said *now.*

Then he kissed her cheek. Her nose. Her chin. When his teeth grazed the side of her neck she lifted off the bed. Gripped his back. And groaned.

Needing more, needing skin, needing to assuage the heat, the joy, the guilt—yes, guilt, for it was there still, a constant companion, a bitter tang to every breath he took—merging inside him, he slid down her body. Nipping at her shoulder, her collarbone, the edge of her bra through her clothes.

She writhed under him, gripping his hair. Guiding him. Fearless. Wanting.

When he reached her belly, he nudged her shirt with his nose, and pressed a kiss to the right of her navel. Then the left. The sounds coming from her making his vision hazy, his body, coiled tight for so long, burn.

When he slid his hand beneath her shirt, meaning to ease it away, she pulled the hem back down.

When he tried again, she wriggled out from under him and flipped him over. Straddled him. Her hot wild gaze drinking him in. Eating him up.

Something in her eyes made him pause. Some flicker of doubt. But considering all the big emotions he was grappling with, he couldn't blame her.

"Aubrey, we don't have to—"

Then she tucked her hands into her hair, twirling it into a knot. Her hips moving against his till his eyes near rolled back in his head. Purely deliberate. Nothing sweet about it. No indecision at all.

He reached for her, his thumbs pressing into her hip bones, guiding. Slowing. Watching her. Watching her eyes, drugged and lush with desire. Rolling with her till her breath hitched, her eyes dragging closed.

Her hands fell to his chest. Nails digging in. Biting her bottom lip so tight he feared she'd draw blood.

When she called his name, a keening desperate plea, he reared up, slid a hand behind her head and captured her mouth. Kissing her slow. Deep. Losing himself. Spiralling.

Oh, hell; the tang of salt. Of iron. He slid his tongue along the seam of her lips, finding the spot she'd bitten swelling already.

"Sean," she gasped, her head tipping back, knees spreading, sliding herself along the erection locked in the confines of his jeans.

Then with a roar that seemed to come from the back of her throat, she pulled back, pressed him to the bed. Pointed at him and said, "Stay." Then she rid herself of her shorts, twirled them around a finger and flung them across the room.

Before he had the chance to even think about laughing, revelling in her abandon, her hands were at his fly, unbuttoning, unzipping, and setting him free.

Fearing it would end before it had begun, he rolled her over, and said, "Stay." He grabbed protection from his side drawer, sliding it on with a speed heretofore unknown.

"Yes," she said, watching, relishing, as if she knew he needed to hear it. "A thousand times yes."

And while it took every ounce of strength he could muster, Sean began to slow. His kisses, his touch, the roll of his hips. To pay attention. To be in this. Before it subsumed them both. His hands learning every inch of her body. Until she breathed when he breathed. Her eyes unable to focus. His name a prayer on her lips.

When he finally slid inside her, she cried out— in pleasure, in relief. The power he'd been holding in check detonated as he was sheathed in her, to the hilt.

Then her eyes found his. Locked on tight as they moved.

Lost, together, to the slide of heat. The flood of sensation. The taste, sweet and spicy. And the yield.

The way she gave of herself and the way she gave in. Accepting and following, open and accepting and demanding, till she dragged him under with her.

Under. And over. And undone.

Aubrey lay sleepily tangled in the sheets of Sean's bed, her head up one end, his up the other. Hand over her heart, eyes closed, she checked in.

Her heart, well, it was taking its time to settle, but no wonder. It had been put through its paces.

At least it felt even, and steady, and strong. In fact, it felt indomitable.

"You awake?" Sean's deep voice crooned from the other end of the bed.

"Almost."

"I was just thinking."

"About?"

"When I saw you sitting on the floor of the museum. Backpack open, back to the room, I figured you were a disaster waiting to happen."

"And now?"

"I'm sure of it." He let out a short sharp breath, lifted up onto his elbow, the sheet pooling around his waist, arms and chest on display. And what a display. "You have a tattoo."

"More than one," Aubrey said.

"Words," he said, pointing to his side. "I didn't stop to read them. Was too busy."

"The fact of which I am most appreciative."

Sean nodded. "You're welcome."

Aubrey pulled down the sheet, and lifted her T-shirt just enough to show the words scrawled across the bottom of her ribs. The shirt she'd managed to keep on the entire time they'd made love, without him making a peep of complaint. Meaning he wasn't a boob man, or he was a man who took consent seriously. Considering the way he'd moved around her body, she figured it was the latter.

Sean leaned over her to read, *"'Be in love with your life. Every minute of it.'"*

"Jack Kerouac."

He took a "Sean moment" before lifting his eyes to hers. "Apt."

Aubrey's smile started behind her ribs. "One of the kitchen staff in the—"

She stopped herself just in time. Feeling all loose and lovely, her brain still a little fuzzy around the edges, she'd been about to say, *In the hospital in Copenhagen*, which would only bring questions. Leading to answers that would change everything. He'd made love to her as if she was strong. As if she was whole. She wasn't giving that up for anything.

She went with "—this place I stayed in Copenhagen, was really into quotes. She'd write them on little notes and bring them to me with breakfast. She could hardly speak English, I can't speak Danish, so I think she found them on Pinterest and copied them out. Some were hilarious."

"Such as?"

"Ah. *'You are the gin to my tonic.' 'Coffee doesn't ask me stupid questions in the morning. Be like coffee.' 'If we're not meant to have midnight snacks why is there a light in the fridge?'*" I quite liked that one too. Just thought it might be a little long for the space."

Sean's smile was indulgent. Delicious. What had she done to deserve ending up in this place with that face? Must have rescued ten, twenty children from a burning building in a previous life.

That's the good. What did you do to deserve the bad?

Aubrey closed her eyes, squeezed the voice out of her head.

"You said there was more than one," said Sean. "Tattoo."

There was. Including one he'd never need to know about. Too much explaining to do there.

That was okay though, right? To keep things from him. It wasn't as if they were promised. They were...having fun. And tattoos that covered scars did not—on the whole—fit into the fun category.

Opening her eyes, concentrating on that face of his, she lifted a foot to show her ankle, and the dragonfly thereupon. Super fun! "I was sixteen, pretended I was eighteen. My mother nearly had a fit, which was, of course, the point. Last of four kids, you gotta do what you gotta do to get the attention."

Sean took her foot in hand, pretended to pay the tattoo close attention. All the while his thumb pressed into the soft arch of her foot, making her groan.

Then he pressed his lips to the tattoo, before making his way down her leg. Or was it up her leg?

Whatever.

She closed her eyes, lay back on the bed and let him go up, go down, wherever he damn well pleased.

CHAPTER SIX

AUBREY'S PHONE RANG. Video call from Jessica.

She nibbled on her bottom lip, cocked an ear, heard the shower still running.

She wrapped herself in a sheet, rolled onto her tummy, set up her phone on the pillow and answered. Waited for Jessica's sweet face to centre on the screen. The sound of laughter and music blurred in the background.

"Hey!" said Aubrey. "What time is it there?"

"I'm not sure. Midnight perhaps? I'm at a party in Manhattan."

"Wow, you animal."

"Hardly. Jamie had a table at an industry book awards charity thing earlier tonight."

Daisy joined the conversation, pushing Jess into a smaller space on the screen. She rubbed her eyes. "Jeez, girl, it's ridiculous o'clock."

"Sorry but this is important. It's about Vivian."

Daisy went from half asleep to focussed in half a second flat. "Our Viv? Is she okay?"

"Yes. I think so. It's just…" Jessica leaned so close to the screen she was a nostril and half an eyeball. "There have been *rumours*. She signed up to write a book for Jamie's company. An autobiography of sorts. Single woman runs the world type thing. But news just came through that she pulled out, citing ill health."

"Oh, no!"

"Right? Except I'm not sure I believe that's the entire story," said Jessica. "She sent me a strange message earlier tonight."

"Give me a sec." Aubrey minimised their conversation. Checked her phone. There it was. A private message from Viv asking for updates. Saying how much she was enjoying Aubrey's photographs. That it was bringing back memories of a special time she'd spent in Florence when near the same age. How lucky she was to have all three of them fall into her life.

"She doesn't sound unwell. But she does sound…"

"Odd," said Jessica.

At the same time Daisy said, "Like she's been on the herbs."

"I'll call her later," said Aubrey. "I've been in contact with her quite a bit once we figured out she was the one who'd given us our crazy gifts."

"Super," said Jessica. "Let us know what you find out."

All too late Aubrey realised the shower had stopped. The door to the bathroom opened, and in came Sean, a towel draped around his waist.

He gave Aubrey a slow smile, his gaze travelling down her back. After the night spent together, she'd yet to find her shorts.

It registered somewhere far back in her brain that she was in the middle of something, but the rest was completely taken up with ogling the miles of sculpted chest and broad brown shoulders and the smattering of dark hair leading down towards his—

He crawled up onto the bed. His gaze determined. The man's focus was unparalleled. She knew. He leaned down to press a kiss to her mouth, stopping mere millimetres from touchdown.

"Ah, hello," said Sean, his breath sending trails of warmth over her cheek.

"Hi," Jessica's voice whispered from the phone.

Aubrey's face spun to her phone to find Jessica waving, and Daisy with her mouth hanging open.

"I'm Sean," said Sean.

"Jessica."

"Daisy."

Sean clicked his fingers, his face breaking into a rare smile. "Holy hell, that's *Daisy Mulligan*!"

Daisy looked over her shoulder.

Sean laughed. His face creasing into a smile. An honest to goodness grin. The shape of which made Aubrey's heart stop. Not literally of course. Been there for real. Knew the difference. More like from one beat to the next her heart was no longer quite the same as it had been before.

"Well, what do you know?" he said. "I've leave you to it, shall I?"

"Don't leave on our account," Daisy said, while Sean shot Aubrey a look, making sure she knew there would be hell to pay once she got off the phone.

She watched him walk away, his towel slipping a smidge so she could just see the rise of his glorious butt cheeks over the top.

"Who on earth was *that*?" Daisy asked, twisting her face as if trying to see around the edge of the phone.

"Him? Just some guy I picked up in a museum."

As she said the words she regretted them. Jokes aside, it just felt…wrong. He wasn't some guy. He was Sean. Malone. A man she'd wanted to hold, and kiss, and unravel more than she'd wanted to do those things with another living person in the history of her life.

"No, he's not," said sweet Jess, looking highly affronted. "He's the wood guy. The one you looked up online!"

"Oh," said Aubrey. "The wood guy. I *thought* he looked familiar."

Daisy snorted. "Well, he looks fine in a towel, which isn't to be sneezed at."

"To think," said Jess, "when I travel I lose my luggage and get my phone stolen."

While Daisy said, "Look at you."

"Who, me?" Aubrey queried.

"You're all flushed and floopy and…dare I say smitten?"

Aubrey frowned. "Pfft. Not *smitten*. Just appreciative. Of the man's...bits. And ways. And talents. And all that stuff."

"Well, you look happy, which is lovely. It's all either of us want for you. Just..." Jess leaned into the phone to whisper. "I hope you are being... safe."

Aubrey got the implication, but she hid it well. Holding her chin, looking confused as she said, "*Safe?* Whatever do you mean?"

"I mean I hope you were...protected."

"Protected from..."

"Pregnancy! STDs! Did you use condoms?" Jess stated, then sat back and glared at the phone. "There. I said it. Happy now?"

"God, Mum," Aubrey moaned, "you can be so embarrassing sometimes."

Daisy laughed so hard she fell out of the screen.

Aubrey hoped her grin held up. The moment Jessica had yelled pregnancy her insides had twisted in a way they hadn't for days. Not that she could explain it to them. She'd yet to fill them in on the news from her doctor, feeling that once her girls knew it would make it really real.

"On that note, gotta go," said Daisy. "Get back to the party, Jess. See what you can find out about Viv, Aubrey."

"Will do."

Aubrey blew them both kisses then hung up. Laid back. Shook off the malaise the word "pregnancy" might well always and for evermore cause to descend over her, and stretched her beautifully achy body from head to toe.

This was lovely. This was good. This was something she could still take into her new normal. For while it had been some time since she'd salsa'd—horizontal or otherwise—the man's athleticism knew no bounds.

But they *had* been safe. The first time. And the second. Though it was a bit of a blur as it had morphed, blissfully, wildly, and more than a little naughtily into the third. But yep, yep, yep— safety first.

She was naturally small, with frenetic levels of energy, her periods had always been irregular, and the meds she'd been on kept her weight right down, which had made her cycle near nonexistent. Add all the other drugs that had been pumped into her, the coma, the damage—her system was in recovery, and might be for a long time.

She'd taken it all as best a person could. Stubbornly refusing to let it break her.

Hearing, from her beloved psychologist, that despite her recovery, she was to prepare herself for a life in which motherhood, conception, and carrying a child were not on the cards had been brutal. That had broken her. Snapped her in two. She'd researched. Tried negotiating with her doctors. Sought second opinions. And sobbed. For weeks.

Then one day she'd woken up and made plans. To be in love with her life. Every minute of it.

She ran a finger over the ridges of the tattoo, one that Sean knew about, then lifted her fingers to trace the tattoo he did not. Both inked in the sweet spot of time between removal of her pacemaker and just before starting her "vitamins", the blood-thinning meds she was still on today.

Aubrey glanced up to make sure Sean was still out of the room, then she leaned over the edge of the bed, grabbed her backpack, riffling through one of the many pockets till she found her angiotensin-converting enzyme inhibitors.

Her doc had said she could stop before she left. But then he'd wanted her to wait around to see how she went. They'd compromised, her dose as low as it could be. A weaning of sorts, from old life, to fully new.

Yep, she was being super-safe.

By the time they roused themselves to actually leave the house, the team had already arrived. Sean whistled and Elwood uncurled himself from his bed in the cool corner of the kitchen and followed him down to the workshop.

Hans quickly turned the music down and four pairs of eyes landed on Sean. Edgy. Hopeful. Trying to decipher if he was the old Sean, or the one who'd shown up the day before. Without Aubrey there to facilitate, Sean didn't have the language to answer.

"Can you guys watch Elwood today? I'm heading into the showroom. Not sure when I'll be back."

Flora nodded and answered for the group. "Of course, boss."

Sean turned to leave, only for his feet to screech to a halt as Angelina called out, in Italian, "Tell Aubrey the *gelateria* near the Ponte alla Carraia is the best. A bit of a walk but worth it."

He glanced over his shoulder to see Flora glaring at her sister, who shrugged back.

"She's still here, right?" Angelina stage-whispered, as ingenuous as Flora was calculating. "We all saw her earlier."

Old Sean would have frowned and walked away. Not played into the drama. Instead, he gave Angelina a smile and said, "Ponte alla Carraia?"

"Sì."

"I'll let her know. *Grazie.*"

And as soon as he left the room, all four of his crew burst into laughter, the music turned up nice and loud and they got to work.

Once back upstairs he found Aubrey tying up a sandal, her foot on a chair. An early model he'd made in the first year he'd lived in the city. Delicate, diagonal arm rests. Not good enough to sell, but beautiful enough to lead him to the next design that did. In the thousands.

Her hair was tied back in a short ponytail with a big scarf. She'd changed into clothes she must have had in her backpack. Dark denim shorts that showed off every inch of leg. A white T-shirt with *I'm With the Band* scrawled across the front, tied in a knot at her waist. Sandals that twisted up her calf like a Roman soldier's.

Her skin—lightly gilded by the Florentine sun—was shiny with sunscreen. Such an Australian thing to see.

She grinned at him before biting down on a peach she'd nabbed from the bowl on the bench.

"God, you're cute," she said, giving him a lazy once-over.

Sean looked down at his loafers, knee-length khaki shorts, and linen button-down rolled up to the elbows. "Okay."

She sauntered away from the chair, snuck up onto her tiptoes, and grabbed him by the chin, bringing him down for a kiss.

She tasted of toothpaste and peaches and sunshine and sex.

And Sean's mind spun from it.

"You promised me primo tourist stuff. So let's go, boyo." She slung her backpack over her shoulder, the lip closed tightly, for now, and made her way down the stairs towards the informal entrance.

Sean blinked, once again wondering how on earth he'd ended up there. With an impudent, effervescent woman with the most voluptuous ability to seek out joy. She knew Daisy Mulligan, for Pete's sake! Daisy Mulligan, who'd met him while he was wearing nothing but a towel.

Carly would have loved that. He pictured her eyes growing comically wide, as if he'd just told her of his meeting with an actual rock star. If she'd only stuck around long enough to hear it.

"Time waits for no man!" Aubrey called, her voice wafting up from below.

Sean ran a hand over his face, collected himself, called, "Jeez, woman! Give me a minute."

A beat went by before her head popped around the corner of the landing. "You might think I would be offended by that tone, but you should know it actually has me considering forgoing the Uffizi right now, just so I can drag you back to bed." A moment, then, "You are taking me to the Uffizi, are you not?"

"Of course I'm taking you to the Uffizi."

She punched the air, then jogged back down the stairs, her voice carrying behind her. "If you don't hurry I might start doodling pictures on your car!"

He laughed, and ran a hand over the back of his neck.

It would behove him to keep the words he'd heard her say to her friend on the phone—*just some guy I picked up in a museum*—on a loop in his head.

He knew she'd been joking. But there was a truth to it all the same. A truth to hold onto.

"Shall we get a table?"

"It's cheaper if you drink your coffee at the counter," said Sean, nodding at the barista as he got his change for their espressos.

"Seriously? Ha. That's awesome."

Aubrey glanced at the barista, who shot her a flirtatious smile and said, *"Sì. Sei Australiano?"*

"Sì," she said, in affected Italian, smiling back.

While the barista set to making their coffees, Sean fought the urge to drag her out of the café and find coffee elsewhere.

Just some guy I picked up in a museum, he reminded himself.

She was here in Florence on borrowed time. A world trip lay ahead of her. Late the night before she'd told him her plans to ride a camel in Egypt, walk the Great Wall of China, visit Jim Morrison's grave. About how she'd met Vivian Ascot and the unexpected gift that had led her there.

She would meet people along the way. Many, many people. Collecting them like ticket stubs.

The barista said, *"Signorina?"*

She turned to grab their coffees, curtsied her thanks, leaving Sean to muse that Carly would have been smitten by her.

Dammit. He hadn't thought about his sister this much since when it all first happened.

When Aubrey passed him his drink he downed it in one, the fresh brew scorching the back of his throat enough that he coughed.

"Are you okay?" she asked, patting him on the back.

"I thought we didn't ask that."

Aubrey blinked. "You don't. I can ask whatever I want."

He shot her a look, to find her face was sincere. Sincerely adorable. From her upturned lips to her wide whisky eyes, it was a face he enjoyed looking at very much. A face he'd miss when it was gone.

That face broke into a smile, as if she knew exactly what he was thinking.

"Drink up," he growled. "I'm taking you to the Ponte Vecchio."

"Yes! Quick, quick, quick." She sipped and sipped until she'd downed the coffee, then thanked the barista, who gave her another smouldering look.

"Sorry," she said, pointing at Sean with her thumb. "I'm with him."

Then shooting Sean a wink, she led him out of the café.

Two *carabinieri*—Italian police—lounged against the railing at the entrance to what had to be one of the most famous bridges in the world, chatting to tourists.

"Are they for real?" Aubrey said, gaping.

"What?" Sean asked.

"The knee-high black boots, fitted black pants, the hats sitting jauntily on the backs of their heads; they look like Italian Chippendale dancers. I have to get a picture."

She ran up to the pair, waited till they'd finished giving instructions to the tourists before her, and then motioned the international signal for selfie.

Grinning, they held out their arms and welcomed her. She snuggled in between them, imagining how Daisy and Jessica and Viv would love the picture.

"Here," said Sean sidling up to them. "Let me."

Handing over her phone, she splayed her now spare hands at her sides, imagining it looked as if she were gripping the young police officers' thighs. By the twitch in Sean's cheek as he took the photo she figured she was right.

"Grazie," she said, when they were done.

Both men doffed their caps and said, *"Prego."*

She ambled over to Sean, who was holding out her phone. "What?"

He herded her onto the bridge proper. "I didn't say a thing."

"And yet I can feel it. The waves of jealousy pouring off your skin. You have nothing to worry about. I am all yours. Here." She reached out and wrapped her hand around his.

He looked down at it, as if it was something entirely foreign.

And she felt a sudden wash of vulnerability. Heat flashing along her cheeks at the very real fear he give her a look that said, *Honey, that's not what we are.*

Instead he shifted his grip so that he held her more fully, then looked ahead, along the bridge, and began to walk.

Relief flooded through her, brisk and cool. And disturbing. So they'd slept together. In between splendiferous bouts of not sleeping together. But nothing had changed. Not really. They were still ships passing in the night.

"See those tunnels above?" Sean said.

Aubrey pretended she'd been listening, not having a quiet panic. "Mm hmm."

"That's called the Vasari Corridor. Built by the Medici family, so that they could cross the river on horseback high above the rest of the riff-raff. The bridge itself used to be the place to find a good butcher, but the Medicis didn't like the smell, so they moved in jewellers instead, and that's how it remains today."

"Did you know all that, Malone? Or did you do some research some time over the past twelve hours, knowing you were bringing me here?"

Sean's pause told her all she needed to know.

She took her hand and slid it into his elbow, snuggling herself tighter. And he let her. She felt a little bittersweet as they ambled along the bridge, pausing to window-shop. And to talk to anyone who caught Aubrey's eye. She loved finding out where people were from, why they'd chosen Florence of all the places in the world to visit, and what one thing she had to see before she left.

In one jewellery shop a single chair sat in one corner, with what looked like a real fur pelt draped dashingly over the corner. Aubrey ducked inside, went straight up to the chair and checked the back to find the mark she was looking for.

"I knew it! It's a Malone! Did you know this was a Malone chair?" she asked the young woman behind the counter, who gave her a surprised smile.

"Mi scusi?"

Sean moved in, his hands going to Aubrey's shoulders as he attempted to herd her away. "It's a reproduction. A wholesale piece. Likely picked up from a furniture store in town."

"Well, it's still lovely."

"Thank you. I try."

"He's Malone," said Aubrey. "He designed that chair."

The young woman's gaze moved to Sean and stopped. *"Sei Malone?"*

Sean answered in fast, furious, dashing Italian while the more he said, the more the sales assistant swept her hair behind her ear and nibbled her lip and generally gave every indication she might be about to melt into a puddle of lust on the floor.

Huh. If Sean was trying to get her back for the barista, and the *carabinieri*, then he succeeded. An achy discomfort had swept over her. Which was nonsensical. This was a holiday thing. Which would cease any moment. In fact, she might choose to move on to Rome the very next day, meaning, in all likelihood, she'd never see him again.

Rather than that make her feel better, the achy discomfort only heightened.

"I think it's a sign," Aubrey interjected, "that I need to buy something from this shop. A souvenir to remind me of my days here. So I don't ever forget the time I went to Florence."

Sean laughed. A soft sound of complete understanding. His stunning, darkly handsome face shifting into something infinitely lovely as he indulged her utter lie. She'd never forget. This place or him. And he was self-aware enough to know it.

"She likes you," Aubrey said. "You can get her number if you'd like, for when I'm gone."

The smile disappeared. His eyes hardened. "Thanks, but I'm fine."

Aubrey held up her hands in submission, before pretending to check out the wares. Her mind was buzzing. Her skin felt too tight. And it wasn't the heat. Or her heart. At least not the ball of gristly muscle keeping her alive.

She quickly found something—a small gold ring in the shape of a flower—and paid the sales assistant—a delightful girl named Sasha, who was an only child from a tiny little town in northern Chianti, who worked in the shop while studying commerce at university—before finding Sean outside the shop, hands loose in the pockets of his shorts, leaning against a lamp post, watching the world go by. Nose tipped to the sky, he was soaking up the sunshine on his face as if it had been a long time since he'd noticed there was a sun at all.

He turned, his face relaxed, content. "You good?"

And the superficial ache that had come over her earlier shifted and settled, deep inside. Was she good? Not so much. In fact she believed she might be in quite a bit of trouble.

But she nodded. No need to worry the man.

He held out his elbow. She slid her hand back into the crook.

Things remained quiet as they continued along the bridge. Till another *carabiniere* strolled past. Aubrey *might* have sighed.

And Sean chuckled. "Wait till you get to Vatican City. Their uniforms were designed by Michelangelo himself."

Vatican City. Could you imagine? Only she'd have to leave this place to get there. Which was what she wanted. Most of all. To see everything. To open herself up to new experiences so that she might be able to put her old dream behind her and create a new one.

"Now you're just trying to make me self-combust with lust," she joked.

"You do know that's my new mission in life," he said, his voice a low rumble.

She tripped over nothing. Pretended there was a loose paver on the roadway.

Sean's laughter was real. Deep. All hers. And she knew she wasn't going anywhere. Not yet. The Vatican could wait.

Their night together didn't have to be a one-off. Or a three-off, to be fair. She could handle a little more of this, of him, before heading off into the sunset, alone. Couldn't she?

"You can stop the foreplay you know," she said, removing her hand and moving to walk backwards in front of him. Flirtatious. Fun. Keeping things light.

"Is that what this is?" he asked.

And shivers skittered down her neck and into the backs of her knees. "Just take me to the big show, Malone. I need the Uffizi, now, please."

"Done."

"Woohoo!" And as they headed towards the famous museum, Aubrey kept her little shopping bag in the hand nearest him. Figuring it best to keep her hands to herself. For now.

Aubrey was like a cat on a hot tin roof on the walk to the Uffizi Gallery, chatting ten to the dozen and keeping just out of reach.

When all Sean wanted to do was touch her. Fix her scarf before it fell out of her hair. Hold her backpack. Duck into any one of the dark alcoves they passed and kiss her till her hands gripped his shirt in order to stay upright.

"I have to find *The Birth of Venus*. It was commissioned by one of the Medici family for their cousin, did you know? Mine's lucky to get a text on his birthday. And Caravaggio's *Medusa*. My first ever commission was painting my version of the Medusa on the bonnet of my boyfriend's beat-up Corolla."

"You've done your research too, it seems."

"I had a bit of spare time up my sleeve of late. Reading about all the places I could visit kept me sane."

"Then why did you let me go on and on about the bridge?"

"I like your face when you talk about this city. You're so serious most of the time, but when you forget to brood, when you actually start to enjoy yourself, you become quite animated."

"I do not."

"Okay." A few beats slunk by. Then, hovering closer, she murmured, "You're like a little kid, pointing out all the things he wants for his birthday."

With a growl Sean took his chance, finding her hand and twirling Aubrey back into his arms. She laughed as she grabbed onto him. Such easy release. And now he had her, her hand slid over his shoulder and into the back of his hair, the other curled around a button on his shirt.

He wondered if she even knew how she curled into him. Locking herself into place. As if once she had him she didn't want to let go.

"One of these days," said Sean, his voice a low growl, filled with heat and want and all the possessive feelings she brought out in him, "you will mock me one time too many, then look out."

Something flickered behind her eyes. Something wrong. Sean moved to assure her he was kidding, that he'd never hurt her, when he realised that wasn't her concern.

One of these days, he'd said. As if she were sticking around. When she'd been at great pains to make it very clear she had miles to go before she slept.

Which was the only reason he'd let her in. Let her deep. So fast.

Because when she left it would not be a shock. It was a given. Built in.

He reached up and ran a thumb over the creases above her nose. "You can relax, Trusedale. I am well aware that one day I will wake up and you'll be gone. And that my life will have to go on as it did before, only with a you-sized hole in it."

Blink. Blink-blink.

She took longer than usual to compose herself, but her chin did finally lift. "Good. Because that's *exactly* how it's going to happen. Though

I'll probably get my foot caught in a sheet, and make a right ruckus when I hit the floor, busting my knee. So you'll have to pretend you're asleep, okay? So as to allow me to limp out the door with a modicum of grace."

"I can do that."

"Wait, I'm not done."

Of course not.

"You must then fall into a deep depression, for a week, maybe two, when you realise how much you do in fact miss me. But you'll come out the other end a new man. Forged in the fires of my condescension. You name a chair after me. Perhaps a whole collection. Then—"

Sean kissed her to stop her talking.

It was the only way.

His hands to her cheeks, holding her close. He kissed her and she kissed him back. The sun warmed the back of his neck. The sounds of the crowd milling past them—all wolf whistles, and laughter—was a hazy soundtrack to the feel of the woman in his arms.

He pulled back to find her eyes fluttering open. Oaken eyes. So full of truth and heat and questions. Always with the questions.

Dangerous questions. Questions that he could not... *Would not* answer.

How could he whisper in her ear that she made him feel both light and full, human again, that he felt something akin to *happy* for the first time in years, without her misunderstanding? He didn't have the capacity to keep this level of contentment going.

Her eyes flickered between his, searching, before she slowly let him go and took a step away. Her face unreadable, for once. Her eyes distant.

"Oh, look," she said, breaking away.

In the nearest nook was a short tunnel, the ceiling trailing in ivy, and at the end a gate. She gave it a shake.

"Aubrey," Sean warned, "you can't go in there. It's private."

Aubrey gave the lock another jiggle and it sprung open. Her eyes, when they met his, were daring, and a little sharp, as she said, "Live a little, Malone."

Live a little. When he'd been doing his very best to live as little as humanly possible. Stopped by how freaking unfair it was his sister no longer got the chance to live at all.

She stepped through the gate.

And it was his turn to follow her.

Into a tiny courtyard surrounded on three sides by the backs of stone buildings, typical of the area. Tins of paint were stacked under a small awning of one building. Washing hung over the railing on one. Not much in the way of beauty, pure utilitarian.

And yet Aubrey moved to a small stone wall and grabbed her sketchbook out of her backpack.

Then, crouched like that, she set to copying some intricate designs etched into the stones.

"You do realise *The Birth of Venus* is three minutes from here," Sean said.

"I know. But how is this not as valid? Just because some old white guy didn't commission another white guy to carve it, what makes that picture of—?" She leaned closer, her hair falling half over her face as she got a better look.

When she sat up, her lips were caught between her teeth.

"You were saying?"

"Fine. Yes. In amongst the curlicues is the carving of a penis. But it's still art. There's another one. They're everywhere." She looked around at the buildings, the light in her eyes dancing. "Oh, my gosh, how brilliant. Do you think the people who live here know? Do you think they've ever noticed?"

Sean ran a hand over his face. Then coughed out a husky laugh. "You are a true original, Aubrey Trusedale."

"I try," she said, before going back to sketching her own version of the "art". Focussed on that the joy of it.

And Sean figured focussing on joy just a little more, for another day or two, surely couldn't hurt.

In bed that night Aubrey drew circles on Sean's chest, her gaze following the glint of the delicate ring she'd bought on the Ponte Vecchio. Loving it when the ring caught on a hair and Sean flinched.

Proving he wasn't completely unreal.

She was becoming unduly fascinated by him. There were the oodles of lust to contend with, yes. But it was his layers, his edges, his choices that really had her caught. That was what kept her spinning about his axis. Locked in his orbit.

The wondering.

One of those wonderings was how hard it might be to spin away. When the time came.

The thing she was realising was, with the luxury of time and money, there really was no rush. She hadn't made further bookings, or set plans. Viv owned the hotel she was staying in, and when Aubrey had messaged to let her know she might stay longer than originally intended, Viv had insisted she stay as long as her heart desired.

She was travelling to follow her curiosity. To forge a new life path for herself. And right now she was curious about Sean Malone. And all the ways he could make her sigh. All the ways he made her feel so very alive.

Her senses were open as they'd never been opened before. She could see colours, pick out aromas, feel textures, enjoy sitting and breathing in a way she'd never been able to do. First because she'd been in an all fire rush to grow up, always looking forward, and then because she'd been spending every spare second trying not to die.

Or maybe it was all Sean Malone.

For all the amazing things she'd see and do on this trip, she knew she'd never forget the sound of his voice. The deep, rough burr; never raised, but often exasperated. Calling her name from another room. Murmuring on the phone. Making grand promises in her ear and then, oh, the follow through.

She might have tugged a little hard, for Sean's body jolted beneath her touch.

Oh. She'd put him to sleep. That wasn't going to do her any good.

Another tug and he woke with a snuffle, his head tipping to face her, brow furrowed. The moonlight pouring through his huge windows creating slashes of shadow and light across his beautiful face.

"Did you just pinch me?"

Aubrey nodded. Slowly. Then leaned over him to kiss the spot.

"You're gonna wear me out, Aubrey Trusedale."

"Maybe," she said, rolling onto her back as he slowly moved over her, "but it'll be totally worth it."

CHAPTER SEVEN

A WEEK WENT BY, then another. Working hard and stealing time to scout out new places in the city to explore with Aubrey, Sean found a balance he'd never thought achievable. Not for him.

"Hey," Sean called, his phone open on the webpage he'd been scrolling through. "I'm thinking of trying this new restaurant someone has opened not far from here."

It was a little kitsch. Set up to feel like a dinner party, with everyone eating around the one big table. When Sean had read about it a couple of weeks back, just before he'd met Aubrey in fact, he couldn't think of anything worse than having to make polite conversation with strangers. But Aubrey? It would be her bliss.

So long as he was beside her, his knee nudged against hers, his hand along the back of her chair, good food on the plate, knowing they were five minutes from home, from his waiting bed, he could handle anything.

"Aubrey," he called, not finding her in his bedroom, though the en suite bathroom door was ajar, the light on.

"What do you think of this?" he said, pushing the door open a smidge to find her, hands gripping the edges of the sink, head slumped. Her bohemian yellow top had slipped off one shoulder, the blade poking out sharply. The veins in her arms struck blue in her pale skin.

"Aubrey," he said, hearing the thread of dread in his own voice and not liking it one bit.

She looked up, catching his eye in the mirror. And what he saw there made his stomach muscles clutch. Fear, pain, and concealment battled in her gaze. Swimming over the top, like living mercury; her silent pleas that he not ask if she was okay.

For a moment—a heartbeat—he considered backing out and closing the door. Giving her the privacy she clearly wanted.

It was the easier move. The one with the best chance at salvaging some form of self-containment.

But he'd been there. Opted to trust. To respect boundaries.

And lived to regret it.

He pushed the door open with more force than he'd intended. And found himself asking words he'd never wanted to utter. "Aubrey, what's going on? Are you...sick?"

She flinched. Then, with a stubborn lift to her jaw, said, "I'm fine."

Sean looked closer, taking in the dark smudges under her eyes. Wisps of her hair curled against her forehead, as if she'd been sweating. And a whole bunch of small signs he'd blithely let slide coagulated into a telling tale.

"The vitamins you claimed to be taking… They're not vitamins, are they?"

"Have you been through my stuff?"

"Of course not. Have you been lying to me?"

She flinched again. As if she was barely holding herself together.

Her phone rang right at that moment. A picture of a smiling couple, the ID reading *Mum and Dad*. Without a pause she sent it to voicemail and turned her phone over. Other times, when he'd found her talking quietly on the phone, she'd signed off as soon as she'd spotted him.

He'd thought she didn't want whoever was on the other end to know about him. Now, he realised, she didn't want *him* to know about *her*.

"Aubrey, you're so pale I can see through your skin. Talk to me. Tell me what's going on."

A muscle flickered in her cheek. Her lean shoulders squared. As if she was preparing to take him on. Or run.

But she stayed, catching her own eye in the mirror, shaking her hair off her face, attempting to rally. "There's plenty we don't know about one another and that's okay. We've made no promises, Malone. This has all been so lovely. Fun. Light. And I know you'd rather keep it that way."

It was his turn to flinch, at her assessment of his character. But she was right. Or he would have said so only a few weeks before.

But now, the not knowing, the keeping everything locked up tight, it didn't sit right. It felt shallow. And it felt untrue.

"My name is Sean."

She blinked. Her brow furrowing.

He moved deeper into the bathroom to stand beside her, leaning a hip against the bench so she had to look at him directly. Not through the haze of the mirror.

"I was named after my grandfather, the one who taught me woodwork. My middle name is Eric. I had a lisp until I was ten and my front teeth grew in. I didn't learn to drive till I was twenty-one because I lived in uni housing so had no need. I haven't spoken to my parents in over a year. Before that I ignored their calls, emails, and carrier pigeons for as long as I could before checking in. Even then the contact was brief, loaded with agony as we've known tragedy in our family and the only way I knew how to deal with it was to put it behind me. Literally. And I know why you call me Malone."

She looked like an animal, trapped, all wide eyes and fidgets.

He knew, as deep down inside as he'd ever let himself see, that she needed this. She dreamt of jumping out of a plane over the desert, swimming with sharks, and already she talked to any stranger who caught her eye. But, he was coming to realise, intimacy, revealing the parts of herself she believed people might not find so charming, scared the hell out of her.

Seeing her tremble and sweat overrode every instinct to turn his back. To not become involved. He held out a hand. "Come with me."

While her innate stubbornness rolled in, like a storm over the ocean, she eventually turned and put her hand in his.

He took her into the bedroom, motioned for her to sit on the end of his unmade bed, the sheets still tangled from a night in her arms.

She sat, tucking her hands beneath her, her pinkie fingers poking out from beneath the hem of her short denim skirt.

From a drawer in his clothes chest—beneath his spare change, scraps of notepaper and passport, as if it were so much detritus—Sean found a small photo album.

His mother had had it made. A copy for her, a copy for his father, and a copy for him. He knew she'd done it in some effort to help. To show them all that the good years had far outweighed the one year of truly bad.

But it had only pressed home how deeply, how unutterably, he'd failed.

Curling his fingers around it for the first time in years, he moved to the bed, sat beside Aubrey. The spine of the album made a cracking noise as he opened it up.

The first picture was of him—kindergarten

age—wearing a cowboy outfit for his fifth birthday party, his mum and dad's faces pressed up to his cheeks. His hair was lighter, his eyes brighter. He looked happy but ready to bolt from the frame to join his friends on their bikes.

Aubrey's finger hovered over his face. Then those of his parents. "Your mum… She looks like she could eat you up. And your dad's hot."

A laugh rose inside, but was quickly snuffed. He knew what she was trying to do. Her humour was her secret weapon for keeping intimacy at bay.

Sean flipped the page. Next came a picture of him at around age eight. A little girl with pigtails hugged him like there was no tomorrow.

"Who's that?"

"That," said Sean, running a thumb over a smudge on the page, "is my sister, Carly."

"Carly. Have you mentioned a sister?"

Her words didn't have their usual bite. Either she was too exhausted by whatever it was that had her slumped at his side, or she knew him well enough to understand he wasn't sharing this lightly. That now was not the time to mock.

"I haven't. I don't talk about her. Or my family. If I can help it. It's…difficult. Carly died; a little over five years ago now. Drug overdose."

"Oh. I… I have no idea what to say."

And so she said nothing. Simply encouraged him to turn the pages. There he was, throwing

Carly in the pool. The two of them at a restaurant somewhere—Carly's eyes crossed, his cheeks puffed out like a blowfish. The photo of him in the shed felt like yesterday; looking earnestly at their grandfather while they worked on some basic lathing, while Carly lay outside, sunning herself, reading a book.

The last photo had been taken about six months before Carly died. It was a candid shot of the family at a trade show in which one of his chairs—a fluid, sweeping, laid-back cantilever that seemed to defy gravity—had won a big prize. It was during the time Sean had believed she was better. But in the photo it was clear she was not. The light in her eyes was dimmed, her cheeks sallow, her fingers curled into claws as she fussed with her bitten-down fingernails.

Aubrey's head slowly moved to lean against his upper arm. A warm body at his side. And it was enough to loosen the perpetual tightness in his throat.

"I was the firstborn. A good kid. Always doing the right thing. Making good choices. Good grades. My friends were all honour students, athletes, achievers. Carly was always wild. And brave. A daredevil. A risk taker. It enticed a darker crowd. Kids who craved attention from the shadows. But even as she began to change, to move away from us, to me she was always Carly. My brilliant, bratty little sister.

"When I went away to uni things got bad, fast. Drugs. Petty theft. A guy who didn't treat her well. Chatting with Carly, she seemed fine. Brushed it off as a little light rebellion. My parents—who are not the kinds of people to show when things are hard—didn't even let me know how bad things were till the night they came home to find their front window broken, their TV missing. They didn't need to beg me to come home. I came. Instantly.

"Carly seemed to rally, having me around. I was her ballast. No judgement, with me she could take her time to find her way back. She could breathe. She dumped the guy. She held down a job. We all had dinner at our parents' place three times a week.

"I got more and more antsy at being home. I'd given up my degree. All my doer friends were off doing and I was playing babysitter. As for the family dinners—the best thing I can say about them is they were polite, three courses, and on time. And Carly seemed better. My business was taking off. I revelled in being busy. I became less available each day.

"I figured my parents would let me know if things began to shift off course. But they, being the kind of people they are, again tried to shoulder it on their own.

"My little sister was twenty-three when she died. OD'd at a party held in an abandoned warehouse on pills she'd robbed from a pharmacy with her junkie ex-boyfriend."

As he said the words, Sean felt a fog shift over him. His voice, to his ears, coming from a mile away. Then he felt Aubrey shift beside him. Heard her sniff, before her hand moved to quickly swipe at her eye.

He slowly closed the album. And looked at her. Waited till she looked at him.

"I won't do that again, Aubrey. I won't deliberately put myself in a position where I can be sideswiped. Tell me about the pills."

Her eyes, red-rimmed and wholly devastated, looked deeply into his own. This woman who adored hearing people's stories, who absorbed them like warmth from the sun, was hurting. For him.

The urge to reach up and cup her cheek, to kiss away her tears, to own her pain, was overpowering.

But he had worked too hard to create a life in which his responsibilities were simple and clearcut. In which he did not take on more than he could bear to lose.

The wound of losing his sister still burned— open and feral and for ever. And the guilt... The guilt had stripped him bare.

Realising, then, how much he'd let slip these past few weeks, how easily she'd found a way in, he hardened his heart before saying, "Tell me now, Aubrey, or I'll call a car to take you back to the hotel. And that'll be it. I won't see you again."

"Wow," she said, the warmth in her eyes cooling, as if she was adding a few new walls herself. "You're sexy when you're bossy."

"Aubrey—"

"Okay! Okay. Okay."

She pushed herself off the bed, went into the bathroom, rummaged around in her backpack and came back with the little container in which she kept her "vitamins".

She rolled the bottle in her hand a few times, before handing it over.

A lot of chemical gobbledygook and brand names with *angiotensin converting enzyme, ACE, inhibitors* written in bold.

From what little he knew of such things an inhibitor reduced or suppressed...something. Was it a thyroid thing? Something as simple as that?

"I'm not a chemist, Aubrey. You're going to have to translate."

"Angiotensin converting enzyme inhibitors relax the blood vessels so that the heart doesn't have to work quite so hard."

Her *heart*? The hardness around his own took a hit. "And why would your heart not need to work so hard?"

She looked down at her hands, her fingertips and thumbs running over one another in a nervous dance. Then she breathed out hard and said, "A couple of years back, right after the music festival in Copenhagen, in fact, I collapsed. I ended up in a Danish hospital for several weeks while they tried to figure out why. They were stuck on believing I'd taken something at the show, you see. That it was an allergic or toxic reaction to some dodgy ingredient cut into some dodgy drug."

Aubrey shot him a look then, piecing together his story with hers. Her eyes filled with mortification and sorrow. "It wasn't like that! I promise. I'm not into that kind of thing. A cocktail, yes. But before the collapse I'd avoid even taking paracetamol."

Sean said, "I believe you. Go on."

"My parents did what good people do and listened to the doctors. When questioned, as I lay on a ventilator by that stage, they admitted I was headstrong. A little wild. Not so good at following rules. They…believed it was my fault."

Sean's fingers curled into fists in the effort to sit still and listen. To not react. Or comfort. Or cut his losses and walk away.

"Anyhoo, since they were on the wrong track, I went downhill fast. Ended up in the ICU. Even an induced coma for a period before they diagnosed me as having myocarditis. My heart, by that point, had taken a beating. I went into heart failure."

Sean's eyes felt so gritty, he forced himself to blink.

"My folks… They've never forgiven themselves

for not trusting me. Not pushing harder, faster, for a correct diagnosis. Then they started blaming themselves. Figured it was something to do with the paint we used at the shop. That they hadn't provided good enough safety equipment. Or the right size.

"Truth was I'd not told anyone about the shortness of breath, or the occasional missed heartbeats I'd felt leading up to that day, figuring it was down to excitement that I was finally heading off on the trip I'd been saving for since I sold my brothers' Lego to other kids at school when I was eight years old. I didn't want anyone to tell me if I was sick I couldn't go. But turns out I had a virus. The virus caused the myocarditis.

"They pumped me full of all kinds of gear—anti-viral corticosteroids, inhibitors, beta blockers, now the meds to reduce the risk of blood clots forming in my heart. I'm only on a tiny dose now, working towards coming off them, which is great. But—"

After a few long seconds, Aubrey pulled down the top left shoulder of her shirt and he finally understood why she'd never removed her shirt any time they'd made love.

There was a scar, about an inch long, just above her heart. And above it? A tiny tattoo, etched along the top. The zigzag of a heartbeat, looping into a broken heart, then a zigzag again.

"I had a mechanical pump inserted inside me

for a while, until they decided I wasn't in need of a transplant. Then I went home. Not well enough to drive, work, go out and be in the world for months. Can you imagine? Me cooped up? On bed rest?"

Sean attempted an expression that showed he understood, but he was still attempting to absorb the image of the scar; puckered, pink, and clearly recent.

"So I hunkered down. I ate my veggies. I did my rehab exercises. Saw a psychologist who helped me more than anyone. Dry wit. Honest. Gave me great practical tools. I loved her. Till she told me I can't have kids."

Aubrey said the words in the same tone as if she were telling him a funny story about one of her nephews, but her body… She all but crumpled before him. Her face falling into her hands.

Sean's next breath squeezed from his lungs. He wished he'd never found her in the en suite bathroom. That right now he was booking dinner someplace light. And fun.

And yet…

Knowing this, knowing her truth, having shared his, everything had changed. He felt in it now. Grounded. The urge to keep moving, doing, exploring, to stay out of his own head simply dissolved away.

"Aubrey," he said. "Sweetheart. It's okay. You don't have to say any more."

"No!" she said, sitting up, her eyes a liquid gold

as they held onto his. "I want to. I have to. It's like an animal trying to claw its way out of my chest."

"Okay then. Let it out. I can take it." It was his turn to absorb her story. As best he could with his limited experience. His limited means.

She nodded. Licked her lips. "She told me that having children… They never say never. Fear of getting sued, I guess. She said the chances are infinitesimally small. She gave me pamphlets about freezing eggs, and egg donation, and the legalities of surrogacy. I'm for all that. Whatever it takes for a family to have a kid or a kid to have a family. It's just… The dream I had of *my* future was so simple. It didn't seem like too much to ask. And to be told no. Just no. It…it's been challenging to see the way forward."

"Tell me about it," said Sean. "Tell me your dream."

Aubrey looked at him anew. Her brow furrowing. As if she was trying to figure out if he was merely indulging her. Then she looked up at the chandelier hanging over his bed, and breathed out a shaky sigh. "You, with your grand life, you'd think it was silly."

"Not a chance. I promise."

And so she told him. Travel, a nice guy, house, yard, kids. Weekend barbecues with her brothers and all the nieces and nephews. Grandparents involved every step of the way. That was it.

It sounded…loud, messy and chaotic for a guy

who grew up in a house in which there was no running, no dirty shoes. Where the backyard was a showpiece kept by the gardener, with a sister who was glared at any time she burped at the dinner table. The older he'd become, the more it had felt as if it weren't real, more some halcyon existence people used to sell SUVs and home loans.

"How about you?" she asked, catching him off guard. "Do you want kids?"

His, "No," was quick. And honest.

Even before the shadow of Carly's death, trying to carve out a life of his own, one that felt real, and true, had been challenging without a model on which to base it. The thought of bringing kids into that felt unfair.

For Aubrey, he gentled. "I didn't grow up with the same kind of family you did. Our life was more…structured. Composed. Less barbecue, more dress for dinner. I like kids. I was one once, if you can believe that. But after Carly… I just don't see how parents do it—live with the fear, every second, that no matter what they did it could still end in tragedy."

Aubrey blinked. "Hate to tell you, but that's Parenting for Beginners. My oldest brother still holds a mirror to his son's sleeping mouth to check he's breathing before he himself goes to bed."

"Was that meant to change my mind?"

"No," Aubrey said, letting go a laugh that was more of a sob.

Then she reached over, and took his hand. Hers was small. Cool. He curled his fingers around it. She waited till he looked her in the eye.

Her eyes were clear. So clear he felt he could see a mile past the surface, right into her deepest depths. To find someone complicated. Searching. Determined. Kind. Empathetic. And drawn to him, still.

"Don't want kids if you don't want kids. Just don't be a fatalist," she said, her voice no longer wavering. "It doesn't suit you."

"Then what does suit me?"

"Linen," she shot back without pause. "Those jeans, the dark ones, that hug your backside just so. The colour blue. The look you get when you think I don't know you're watching me. All hot and simmering, full of ideas of what you'd like to do to me when you next get me alone. I like that on you best of all."

She nudged him with her shoulder, trying to perk *him* up.

Sean snuck a finger under her chin, tilted her face till she looked him in the eyes. "What do you need me to do?"

Her mouth opened, and closed. "Not a single thing. This has been perfect. Lovely. Magical. You, Sean Malone, have been an antidote."

Sean's fingers slid around the edge of her chin. His thumb tracing her jaw. "That's right, you're using me."

"I'm totally using you. And don't you forget it."

Something shifted in the air in that moment. Like an invisible string curling around them.

"The thing is though, Aubrey, I know you like to take on the world as if daring it to even try and stop you. But you're not invincible. None of us are. It's okay to make mistakes. To take a day. It's okay to slow down."

A smile flickered across her full lips. "I know. I do. Just—"

"Just?"

"If you treat me differently after this, Sean, as if I'm some fragile flower, I'm not sure I'll handle it."

"Never."

"You sure? First time I saw you I thought, *Hot damn.* First time you saw me you thought, *She's gonna be mugged.*"

That was true. But hot damn had followed right on after for him too.

"I will never treat you as if you are a fragile flower," he said. "I promise."

She swallowed, her eyes locked onto his. Fierce and damaged. Wary but warm. The most beautiful contradiction he'd ever known. And those eyes—those brimming oaken whisky eyes—drank him up. He'd never in his life had anyone look at him the way she did.

And Sean felt the last vestiges of the protective shell around his iron heart shudder and shift, dissolving in places, floating away in others, not sure if he'd ever be able to re-forge them again.

Then she straightened her spine, leaned into him, and lifted to gently press her lips against his. She kissed him softly, again and again, until he had no choice but to kiss her back.

It was an elixir. She was an elixir. A giver of life. But he had been empty for so very long, his well dry, he did not want to deplete her.

So he broke the kiss. Pulled away.

She rested her forehead against his chin. "That was intense."

"Little bit."

"Let's say we don't do that again for a while."

"What's a while?"

A single shoulder shrug, her shirt falling a little further down her arm. "Not sure. A bit longer. Maybe. If it's still okay with you."

"Sure. Why not?"

"That's the spirit." She moved up onto her knees, straddling him. Both hands on his shoulders, she gave him a shove, pushing him back onto the bed. Then she leaned over him, lips hovering just over his. "You and me, we are both allowed to make mistakes. We are both allowed to take a day. And we could both do with a little fairy dust."

Another kiss, deep this time. Her warm body melting into his.

Sean's arms went around her, his hands sliding

beneath her loose top and up her bare back to find her hot, lush and a little sweaty.

She pulled away, panting slightly, her eyes dark and determined.

"Let's agree, here and now, to be one another's fairy dust. To keep this thing easy and light. A holiday fling. No promises, no debts. No knight-in-shining-armour concern for my busted heart. Trust me when I say I've got this. I'm all over it. I'm *fine*. Is *that* okay with you, Sean?"

"It's okay with me." Heaven help him, as he said the words he'd half believed them.

Till she had to go and call him by his name.

Not Malone. Sean.

He slowly rolled her over, till they were side by side, legs intertwined. "Show me your tattoo again."

"What? No."

"No promises. No debts. But no more secrets either. Show me."

Nostrils flaring, eyes brimming with vulnerability, she slowly pulled down the neckline of her shirt to reveal the tattoo. And the scar.

His heart, now unprotected, beat hard against his ribs. "Does it hurt?"

She shook her head, not meeting his eyes. "It can pull a little. Can be tender when it's cold out."

And while the thought of why it was there tore at him, his anger was stronger still. That someone so lovely and kind and bright could be so struck. Could feel untethered for so long.

Breathing deep, he leaned down and kissed her, just above her scar, on the tattoo she'd been too afraid to let him see lest he treat her as if she was breakable. Right on her broken heart.

She shuddered.

When he pulled back tears were streaming down her face. Emotion so raw and real it was more than he could hope to name. And while it felt light years beyond easy, beyond light, beyond a holiday fling, he drew her to him, anyway, losing himself in her.

They never made it out to dinner.

The next morning, Aubrey woke to find herself alone in bed.

Mind you, it was nearing ten in the morning, after an emotionally exhausting night, followed by the most wonderful, tender, glorious make-up sex.

The sound of whirring machinery told her there was work afoot deep below the villa.

She stretched herself out to the four corners of the bed, groaning as bits and pieces of The Conversation came back to her. For all the lovely that had come after, it had been so hard admitting the truth of her condition to Sean.

Finding out could have easily been a tipping point for him. The man was a grown-up. With strong opinions. And limits as to what he would accept. And she'd pushed those limits pretty hard. Regards his staff. And the people in the laneway. And his family.

She groaned, flinging her arm over her eyes.

What a fool she'd been.

Not only to assume his greatest benefits were his pretty face. And clever hands. But to suggest they agree, out loud, to keep things easy and light, no promises, no plans.

When her feelings for Sean Malone had grown to be anything but easy. Anything but light.

Because last night she'd finally seen into the man's heart. And what a massive beast of a thing it was. Deep, soulful, caring, steadying, protective, understanding. And forgiving. During The Conversation, that strength had more than made up for the restraints of her own faulty ticker.

Despite his own pain, his own self-confessed limitations—and what sounded like some deeply held survivor's guilt—he'd listened, he'd respected, he'd held her close.

Because he cared. For her. Not because she was the kind of girl who'd always had the ability to convince people to do things for her, but because he wanted to. Wanted *her*. More than he wanted the peace and quiet of the lifestyle he'd carved out before she'd stumbled raucously into his life? Maybe. Just maybe.

Holding tight to that thought, she rolled out of

bed feeling…airy. As if a huge burden had been lifted off her shoulders.

After showering and changing and repacking her backpack—having picked up a couple of changes of clothes from her hotel the day before— she opened the bedroom door to find Ben slowly pacing the floorboards as if he'd been doing so for some time.

"Ah, hello?"

He flinched. "Aubrey. Hi. Morning."

"You're not Sean."

"I did mention you might notice that."

Mention. Meaning Sean knew he was there.

Aubrey moved to sneak around Ben, only to have him lean to block her. She held out both hands. "Whoa there, partner. What's going on?"

"Um, Sean has to work today. Commission deadline. Admin. All piled up. I thought… I offered to show you some stuff today. Around town."

"Did you now?"

"Yep." Ben looked up and away, classic sign of lying.

She'd have felt sorry for him if all the lovely, warm, exciting, new feelings she'd been revelling in not that long ago weren't now caught up in a massive messy jumble.

Aubrey slid her phone from the outer pocket of her backpack and called Sean. What would she say when he answered? *Are you avoiding me? Be-*

cause I'm sick? Did the cold light of day bring all we said into sharp, all too real relief?

She swore she could hear the faint shrill of the ringtone from downstairs, yet the phone rang out.

So she typed in a text. Showing it to Ben. "Too much?"

Ben shook his head, then nodded, all while looking as if his eyes were about to bug out of his head.

She hit send.

What's the haps, Malone? You seem to have shrunk. And your hair changed colour. And when I kissed you, you tasted different.

Sean texted right back as if he'd been waiting for it.

Funny girl. I have to work. You have to play. That is how it is written. So I've given Ben the day off to show you his Florence.

Aubrey felt the air leave her nostrils in a frustrated steam. She showed Ben his boss's response. He looked so pale she might have worried he'd faint if she weren't feeling so furious.

"Next time, do a better job of keeping your stories straight, okay?"

"Okay," said Ben.

Aubrey scrunched up her face in chagrin.

"Sorry. This isn't on you. Not your fault your boss is a stubborn so-and-so. And I'd actually love to see your Florence. I'm imagining less walking, less opera."

Ben laughed, then ran a hand up the back of his neck. "I was thinking food and a vinyl-record store I haven't had a chance to check out."

It was enough for her to refrain from showing Ben her next message.

You do remember what happens when men show me their Florence, right?

A few long, heavy beats slunk by as Sean took that one in. His eventual response?

I remember.

As she imagined the word in his deep intimate voice, Aubrey's belly filled with butterflies. Goose bumps skittered all over her skin.

They had something. It was deeper than either of them would admit. And clearly, considering he was giving himself some space, Sean was struggling with it as much as she was. Could she blame him? Should she call him on it? Or give him a day? Give him whatever time he needed?

Sean filled the gap, texting.

Dinner. The best fettucine of your life. I'll tip

the waiter to serenade you. You can even pick the song.

Aubrey coughed out a laugh.

And she closed her eyes as she told her heart to stop fussing and settle down.

Sean was a grown-up. With strong opinions. And limits as to what he would accept.

But so was she.

She ducked around Ben and darted down the stairs to the workshop where she found Flora and Sean arguing. Arms flailing. Boisterous Italian bouncing off the ancient stuccoed walls.

When Flora saw Aubrey she stopped, her face reddening. Muttering, only slightly less loudly than she'd been shouting, Flora threw up her hands and turned away.

Sean spun, his dark eyes catching on hers.

Her heart fluttered, coughed, caught on the look in his eyes. The caution. The concern. Before he blinked and it was gone. His face clear. His expression blank.

"Problem?" Aubrey asked.

"We were just arguing over…the shape of a table leg," Sean assured her.

Flora snorted. And the concerns Aubrey had pushed out of her mind came back with a vengeance.

"Okay, so I just wanted to check in before Ben

and I head off. We're going to have the best time! Right Ben?"

Ben, hovering on the bottom step, muttered, "Um, sure. We'll have a nice time. Average nice. The regular kind."

"Sure you don't want to play hooky and join us, Malone?"

Sean's cheek twitched at her use of his last name. His eyes dark, unreadable. No smile. No mocking come back. No sign of the man who'd held her so close the night before.

"Okay then, bye," Aubrey said, backing away before the tickle in the backs of her eyes turned into something.

As she ducked out of the workshop doors into the light of day, she wished she'd never caught the look in Flora's eyes. Full of sorrow and regret. As if she'd seen this version of Sean before.

Sean followed Aubrey to the double doors leading out to the drive. But even while a thousand words crammed into his throat—from *Wait, I'll take you* to *I am a damn fool*—he said not a word.

He watched as Ben helped her into his Fiat. Watched as she smiled up at the lanky kid. Said something that made Ben laugh. And blush. And run a hand up the back of his neck.

Aubrey did not wave as the car drove away. Or even look back. He could picture her jaw, tight and strong. Her shoulders back and fierce. Her clever

brain ticking over all the reasons he might have
sent her off without him.

"Dammit," he muttered, the word tight in his
throat.

Part of him wanted to message her, to ask if
she had the answer. Because he sure didn't. Not
with any real clarity.

All he knew for sure was that from the moment he'd seen her gripping the edge of the sink
the night before, her face pale, sweat dappling her
brow, something huge had shifted inside him, and
was still shifting. Knocking, crushing, rearrang-
ing him at the cellular level.

After hours of it, he felt a bruising ache. All
over. Every breath hurt. Every feeling stung. The
thought of holding her, agony. The thought of letting her go even worse.

She was right. He *had* sensed it—her fragil-
ity—that first day. For all her strength, her confidence, her determination, it was something she'd
carry with her always. The same way he'd carry
Carly's death.

A shadow. A ghost.

Being with her, letting her light warm him
when he'd been in the cold for so long, he'd been
sure he was inured against her like. That his experience had tempered him to a point of invul-
nerability.

Aubrey was something he'd never counted on.

"Sean?" Flora's voice called, flatly. "Malone." Then, "Boss?"

Sean turned.

"If you're done mooning, can you please give me the instructions you simply had to give me this morning, the ones that were so important you sent Ben in your stead? Or can I go back to doing what I already do perfectly?"

"I… Sure. Maybe."

Flora moved to him, smacked him in the arm. "Focus. If she messes with your head, boss, we all suffer. We need the work, just as you do. So pull yourself together."

"Flora!" Angelina exclaimed, while Hans furiously cleaned the crevices of a turned table leg with a toothbrush.

"He needs to be told!" said Flora. "For his own good! As he looked after us when we needed it most, now it is our turn to look after him."

Sean looked at her, then at his crew, all bar Ben, who was hopefully driving safely down the hill with his precious cargo in tow.

To think, only a few weeks before they'd all been so polite. Yes, boss. No, boss. Three bags full, boss.

Flora would never have punched him, much less roused at him, or sassed him. Now they were all at it. Ribbing him about Aubrey. And castigating him if they thought he could do better. Coming to him with ideas, telling jokes, and sharing their own stories.

Giving him space if he needed it. And a knock to the head if he needed that too.

As if they were family.

Aubrey, he thought, her name a clutch in his belly. Aubrey had done that. The seeds had been there. In the good people he'd chosen to be around. The wish, on their behalf. She'd yanked them all together in a way he'd not had it in him to allow before.

Aubrey, with her scars. Far more literal than his own.

Aubrey, with her already badly broken heart.

He was the one who had to find the strength to let it in. To let her in. Fully. None of this light, easy, no-promises guff.

He had to give this thing a chance, or his actions would be truly unforgivable.

CHAPTER EIGHT

THE NEXT COUPLE of weeks rushed by in a flour-
ish with Aubrey filling two new sketchbooks with
studies of tiles, fabrics, faces and graffiti.

Now that she wasn't in such a rush to do all the
things, she found herself noticing the world in a
different way: flowers and notes tucked into the
carvings in walls, children playing in the streets,
their mothers watering them down with a hose so
that they might ride out the intense heat.

It made her think more and more about her life
back home. And she found herself missing it more
than she'd imagined she would.

She'd started regular video chats with her family. Meaning she'd been able to see how truly well
her parents were doing. How healthy. How happy.
How crazy they were driving her brothers now she
wasn't around for them to concentrate on.

After that first odd morning following The
Conversation, things with Sean had found a new
groove too. In between day trips to trade school
to give guest lectures, phone calls with a couple
of extremely famous movie stars whose Aspen
chalet he was decking out with custom beams, of
all things, he'd found ways to be with her.

Cinque Terre and Siena. A sunrise hot-air balloon over the Chianti region with views to San

Gimignano and the Apennine Mountains. A midnight tour of the Crypt of Santa Reparata. Vespa rides and more museums and galleries and eateries than she could hope to remember.

She'd assured him if the whole famous furniture designer thing ever fell through, he could get a job with Contiki, no sweat. He'd not been impressed.

The days he couldn't get away he continued offering up staff to "hang" with her, despite his promise to treat her just the same. Having met his beast of a heart she knew how hard it was for him not to be a protector.

She could not have faulted him. Truly. He'd even started telling more stories of his life back home. A childhood less warm than her own, but there'd been love there all the same.

And yet there was a teeny little voice in the back of her head telling her to pay attention.

She couldn't shake the sense that a new kind of tension rode him. Different from the one that had kept him in its thrall when they'd first met. Tighter, sharper, more immediate. As if the thing that worried him most now wasn't his past, or an email he didn't want to answer. It was her.

That, plus the fact she had no clean clothes and could rely on the hotel to do her laundry, and how she'd not felt a hundred per cent the past few days, meant Aubrey had spent the last couple of nights crashed out in her neglected hotel suite.

She woke from a nap on her hotel sofa, to the sound of someone knocking on her door.

With a groan she rolled out of bed, and hobbled to the door.

"Sean?" she said as she peered through the peephole to find an eye pressed up to the other side.

A voice call loudly from the other side, "No, darling, it's Vivian. So open up."

Viv? Here?

Aubrey blinked, taking what she would forevermore think of as a "Sean moment" to let things settle in her head, before she whipped open the door.

And sure as toast, there stood Vivian Ascot, billionaire and life-changer, looking resplendent in a draping grey ensemble pant suit, her silvery hair a gravity-defying coiffure, enough jewels bedecking her fingers to sink a ship.

A far cry from the pale, injured older woman Aubrey had first met two years before.

With a laugh, Aubrey threw herself into Viv's arms. "I can't believe you're here! I have to call the others. Daisy and Jess. This will blow their sweet minds."

"Of course, dear, whatever pleases you. But first, I would very much appreciate an invitation inside. My feet do not take to plane travel as they used to."

"Oh, my gosh, of course. Come in! My room is your room. Literally. You own it, after all."

"Well, yes, that's true."

After Viv strode inside the room, Aubrey went to close the door only to squeal when she found the space filled by a man who looked as if he could eat Aubrey's brothers for breakfast.

"That's Frank," said Viv from somewhere inside the suite. "My security."

"Frank?" Aubrey asked, checking to make sure. The mountain nodded.

"Well, then. Come in, I suppose."

Frank did; casing the joint before taking up position by the door, hands clasped in front, eyes constantly scanning, as if some deadly threat might materialise out of thin air.

"Who is this Sean?" Viv asked.

Aubrey turned to find Vivian sitting on the couch, watching her. *How did she…?* Ah, right, she'd called Sean's name at the door.

"He's a…friend."

Though as soon as she said the words they sounded ridiculous. To think she'd tried to talk herself into believing that was the goal. How things had tumbled since; Florentine Fling. now confidant, protector, a pair of warm arms, a listening ear, a lover…

Her head suddenly swam. Her insides felt fluttery. She walked her hands across the backs of the chairs till she found herself a seat.

It's not my heart, a voice said inside her head. *It's not.* She must have got up from her prone position too fast. Though when had she last checked in? Closed her eyes, held a hand over her heart?

The last few days she'd found herself yawning by ten in the morning. Feeling starving hungry or not hungry at all, no in-betweens. Even Sean had noticed. Encouraging her to sleep in her own bed, claiming he needed "a night off from her incessant ravishing" if he was going to function as a human person.

Or she might not have been here to meet Viv at all.

She sat, reached out to take Viv's hand. "I can't believe you're here. I'm so happy you are, but this is surreal."

"Good surreal, I do hope."

"The best surreal!"

"Mmm." Viv's gaze moved to look out of the window, a view of the top of the Ponte Vecchio peeking over the balcony railing. "I haven't been to Florence since I was a girl. About your age, in fact. And it hit me when I last spoke to you that if I didn't come soon, I might miss my chance."

"Oh." Aubrey breathed through a sudden wave of nausea. "I know you insisted you were fine when I nudged, after Jessica mentioned you'd pulled out of the book deal citing ill health. But Daisy said you were a no-show at this year's Annual Ascot Music Festival too. Is everything okay?"

Viv's hand landed over Aubrey's. "I am very

well. I've simply hit a point in my life where I no longer wish to do what people expect of me. I'd rather read a book than write one. I'd rather listen to music than present it. And I'd rather go to one of the most beautiful cities on earth to feel romance again, than go because I have some kind of business opportunity lined up there. Does that make any sense?"

Aubrey smiled. "It makes *all* the sense. No set plans. No expectations. That's exactly how I started this trip."

Viv's clever eyes narrowed. "And you've stayed here, in this one place, far longer than I'd imagined you would."

Aubrey sat up. "I know. Sorry. The hotel room—"

"Is yours. For ever if you want it. You do exactly as you please. You needed space, to breathe, to be, so I gave you that. Beyond that, how you spend the money is entirely up to you." Vivian sighed. "I've so enjoyed living vicariously through you all. I never had daughters to spoil. But this has given me an inkling of what that might have been like."

Aubrey squeezed Viv's hand again.

"What I didn't expect was for you to show me what I needed as well."

"And what's that?" Aubrey asked.

"I'm retiring!"

"I'm sorry. Wait? What?"

"I'm retiring! I'm going to travel, as you have.

Perhaps find a little holiday cottage of my own to do up." Viv's eyes looked a little wild as they landed on Aubrey's things around the room. Her dad's ancient fedora. Her phone with its scratched-up stained glass heart on the case. "I might even start carrying a backpack. Whereabouts might I find one like yours?"

Aubrey's head started to spin, for real. "Um, well, it's actually probably not the best choice. I mean, I love it. But it doesn't actually close properly. Sean, my friend Sean, it drives him crazy. He's constantly having to yank it shut. So there's a good chance your stuff will get pinched."

Aubrey put a hand to her forehead expecting it to be hot. But it felt fine. A little damp perhaps, but no fever.

Viv blinked. "No one will be pinching anything. I have Frank."

"There is that." Aubrey swallowed, her belly turning over on itself. When her phone buzzed she took the distraction gladly. It was Sean. "May I?"

Viv waved a hand and pushed herself to standing. "Answer away. I need Frank to help me call Max."

Max. Viv's adorable little sausage dog, and his bolt from her arms at a music festival in Denmark, were the reason they'd all met.

"Say hi from me!"

She read Sean's message.

Aspen job is coming along well, if you're bored and need company?

She sent him one back.

I've found another friend to keep me entertained. Vivian Ascot just turned up at the hotel!

Now you're definitely mocking me.

Aubrey took a quick selfie with Viv in the background and sent it to Sean. Then to the girls while she remembered. Her head had been so fuzzy and forgetful of late.

Sean's response?

Hallelujah. I was getting pretty sick of you.

Aubrey laughed out loud. The sound reverberating through her till she felt warm and fuzzy all over. For *that* was mocking. Mr Serious cracking jokes at her expense, smiling because she made him feel safe enough to do so, made her poor heart swell.

Aubrey's smile faded, her hand going to her mouth as her whole body seemed to revolt at once.

At which point she ran to the bathroom and threw up.

Aubrey sat in the big empty hotel bath—the only spot cool enough to take the edge off the hot flush that she couldn't seem to break——fully clothed, her phone to her ear, her other hand over her eyes, as she spoke to her cardiologist back in Sydney.

The pregnancy test Frank had managed to source from goodness knew where, and its big blue positive cross, twirled over and over and over in her hand.

"It sounds like plain old morning sickness. You should be just fine," the doctor said. "Falling pregnant was the hard part. But, now you are, so long as you take care and are monitored closely, there is the possibility of a low-complication pregnancy."

Falling. Miracle. Possibility. Complication. Pregnancy.

"Okay," Aubrey said, squeezing her eyes tight to try to keep the words in the right order. "That's a big relief. But, the thing is… I'm travelling, remember? I'm in the first city in a whirlwind world tour."

Travelling because she *couldn't* fall pregnant. On a whirlwind tour in the hopes of finding her *new* normal. Her *new* dream. And she and Sean had taken care. Every time. Hadn't they? Sean *had* joked that the condoms in his beside drawer had been there for some time…

"Ah," said the doctor, "that's right. So I'm taking from that this was unplanned."

"Most unplanned. I'd thought my planning days were done."

"Yes. So did we all. Whereabouts are you?"

"Florence."

"Ah, Firenze. A most beautiful city. I bet you're having a wonderful time. Have you seen the David yet?"

"Of course. And, yes, I *was* having the best time imaginable, till I threw up this morning."

"Yes. Mmm… Look, I'll email you the name of a local specialist, a doctor I met at a conference a year or so ago. Very proficient. Make an appointment immediately. I would also stop taking your ACE inhibitors right away."

"My meds?"

"Yes. I would not recommend taking them while pregnant."

"Right." A beat then, "Might they have… damaged…" Aubrey couldn't even say it. For a woman who'd believed there would never be a baby to worry about, the thought of the tiny little peanut in her belly under stress made her feel faint. And ferocious.

"Let's get you along to the specialist, okay? They can check you out and make a plan from there."

Aubrey nodded, not sure she'd be able to form words.

So no heart meds. And pregnant. In a foreign city. Pregnant by a man to whom she'd promised to keep things easy, and light. A man who had made it all too clear a family was not on the cards for him. With very good, heartfelt reasons why.

She gulped, and looked up at the ceiling to stop

gravity taking a hold of the tears brimming in her eyes. "Should I just go home?"

Even as she said it, she saw the irony. She was travelling to make peace with the life she'd left behind. So she could go home to a bright new future. Only now, the thought of leaving this place, leaving Sean… Sean. Her baby's father. Who didn't want children. It felt as though the future she'd been working towards had just slipped through her fingers. Again.

What a mess.

"Be honest about how you feel. Ms Trusedale, you alone know what you are capable of."

Aubrey pressed her thumbs to her eyes and nodded. When she remembered the doctor couldn't see her, she said, "Okay. Thanks, Doc."

Once they had disconnected, Aubrey looked at her phone's background pic: her brothers' kids, the manic brood of nieces and nephews.

Be honest about how you feel.

She knew her doctor meant healthwise. Cold sweats, overtired, fainting, that kind of thing. But the sentiment was far bigger. How did she *feel* about having a baby? A miracle baby? Especially if it might turn out to be her only chance.

Oh, the bittersweet tumble of feelings that swept through her. Too shocked to dissemble, too raw to lie to herself, she knew how she felt.

She was utterly smitten with Sean Malone.

With his focus, his seriousness, his generosity. The thought of being with him, *really* being with him, as he worked, as he lived in this magical city, surrounded by so much art, beauty, food, friends, warmth, felt doable. Felt like a plan she could get behind.

Now adding a child to the mix. Their child… Aubrey imagined a wavy-haired toddler, playing chase in the orchard. The three of them lying on the grass, eating peaches, and watching the clouds drift by.

That wasn't a plan. It was the fairy tale.

The vision hovered a moment—so fragile yet so real, like blown glass before it started to cool. Then it fell in on itself till it was once more a formless blob.

How could she tell him? For just a second she considered not telling him at all. He was such a strong mix of stubborn and good, not telling him would save him from the guilt that would hound him for not being what she needed him to be. Perhaps she could disappear the way she'd always joked she would.

She could go home, and still probably find a nice, unassuming, indulgent, docile guy she'd imagined she'd end up with. The kind that would always buy her mother the same wine for family get-togethers, who would talk engine mounts with her dad, while she mucked about with their kids in the backyard pool.

Only now *that* life felt like the formless blob.

A life here, with the people she'd grown so fond of, with Sean—it could be so shiny and sparkly and sophisticated and healthy and rich and inspiring and full.

If not for the soulful, deep, serious, stoic, damaged prince of a man who refused to believe he was worthy of happiness.

His problem was he thought he was done. Forged. Fully formed. As if *he* were the one made from marble.

Not over his sister's death. Refusing to forgive himself, or his parents, for the perceived roles they'd played in Carly's unhappiness. He could be an amazing father and partner, thoughtful, protective, witty, and good. If only he weren't so stubbornly resistant to believing in the true capacity of his beastly heart.

What was she going to do?

The hand holding the long white stick with the big blue plus symbol moved to hover over her belly. Where it landed.

She closed her eyes and checked in. But rather than reaching for her heart, she reached for the cells multiplying madly in her womb.

Hey there, little one, she thought. *You hear me, okay? I may be a bit flummoxed right now, but, believe you me, you were made from joy. And you are loved.*

Her phone buzzed. She glanced at it to find

another message from the man of the hour. His fourth of the day.

Sean had sent her a photo of Elwood looking forlorn.

Big guy is missing you. Me? I'm great. Getting so much work done. Tell your famous friend not to rush off.

She laughed. Then choked on a sob.

Hormones? Probably.

Or, more likely, it was the fact that she had finally found a new life's dream. And was about to lose it all over again.

Once Aubrey had called the cardiologist in town, and an obstetrician recommended by her, she dragged her feet into the lounge to find Viv sitting, waiting, hands clasped in her lap. Frank the security guy still stood stiffly by the door.

"Report?" Viv said, all business.

"It went…better than expected."

"Do you know what you are going to do?"

"Right now I'm not sure if I want to sit or stand. Beyond that it's a blur." Aubrey leant her arms along the back of the sofa. "Have you ever been in love, Viv?" Then, "Sorry. That's so out of left field. And an incredibly private thing to ask."

Viv surprised her by saying, "Yes. I have been in love. But only the once. His name was Giuseppe. He was a beatnik, from Rome. We met one long hot summer I spent in Florence."

Oh. "Is that why you wanted me to come here first? You were pining?"

"Don't fret, my dear. I got plenty."

"Did you now?" Aubrey said on a choke of laughter.

Viv flapped a hand over her face. "I've had a fine life. No regrets. For what is the point? Life is a potato—you mash it, make gems, or beer-battered fries. All of which are delicious in their own way."

Viv had a point.

"Last I heard, Giuseppe moved to San Francisco. Became a used-car salesman. Married a good Italian girl. Had eight children. Has a comb-over."

"Oh, Viv," Aubrey said on a laugh. "Perhaps you dodged a bullet. And that's quite a lot of very specific info you have there."

"My private detective is very good. How do you think I kept such good track of you girls all these years?"

"Ah, social media?"

Viv patted Aubrey on the cheek. "So innocent. Now, back to you. When do you see the doctors?"

"Early next week."

It would give her time to take two, three, maybe several more home tests. And figure out how to tell Sean. When the time was right. There was no point concerning him unless it was real. Once the doctor checked to make sure everything was okay.

"Pfft. We'll have none of that." Viv motioned to Frank, who came over with a phone in his meaty outstretched hand. "I'll have you in to see them both this afternoon. What use is a rich fairy god-mother unless she can wave her magic wand when it's most needed?"

This afternoon? That gave her *no* time to figure things out. But it would give her peanut the best chance at starting off on the right foot from this point on. So yes, a thousand times yes!

Aubrey hugged Viv hard. And did not let go till Viv de-stiffened, and hugged her back.

"Are you staying here?" Aubrey asked. "There's a spare room. A couch for Frank. Unless he bunks in with you—"

Viv's eyes nearly popped out of her head. "Frank? He's got to be half my age."

"So?"

The women both looked his way. Only the very slightest widening of his eyes made them both sure he'd heard.

"Point well made," said Viv, "but no. I've al-ways preferred a more mature man. Besides, my Max is still in the jet. Customs wouldn't let him leave the Lear, wretched souls. He'll be fretting for sure. I will go get that sorted, have Frank mes-sage you about your doctor's appointments, organise a car to get you there. Unless your…friend might care to accompany you?"

Aubrey imagined sending *that* message.

Hey, Malone! Wanna pick me up? Gotta go see a cardiologist as I have to give up my meds asap. You'll never guess why! And I have to see a baby doctor! Oh, no, I gave the surprise away! You in?

"Ah, no. No point scaring the guy without actual professional back-up proof."

Viv nodded. Her expression all too understanding. "Then I'll see you in the morning. You can fill me in on your appointments and show me your favourite parts of this beautiful city."

"Would love nothing more."

Once Viv and Frank were out the door, Aubrey shuffled into her bedroom and lay back on the bed, her hand on her belly, the other resting over her heart.

Giving them the chance, the quiet, to get to know one another. For if all went well, they'd be in cahoots the next few months.

Making a baby.

Aubrey caught sight of the cherubs floating about on her ceiling, she felt a kind of peace she hadn't felt in a very long time.

CHAPTER NINE

"THIS," SAID AUBREY as she and Viv—and Frank, with little Max in his arms—turned the corner into the laneway that had become one of her favourite places in the world, "is Via Alighieri."

"How charming. Named after Dante, no doubt." Viv had clearly decided to take her retirement decision to heart, forgoing her smart business suit for jeans, a T-shirt and hair in soft waves. As if she'd looked up *Helen Mirren street style*.

Aubrey wore a floaty halter dress. After the cardiologist had declared her *molto salutare*, in excellent health, the day before, and perfectly able to stop her meds, the OB/GYN had given her a heads-up that loose clothes might help with her unsettled tummy. Because she was most definitely pregnant.

She had a photo in her backpack. A video on her phone. A strong little heart beating away.

Her own heart picked up the pace as they neared the smoky glass window where the name Malone's was etched in gold in a heavy vintage-type font across the glass.

Sean was meant to meet them there in half an hour or so, giving her time to find her feet. Find some words. Let go of Viv.

Not enough time, she thought, her heart beginning to race. *Once he knows, time might be about to run out, for good.*

"So this is my Sean's joint," she said.

Viv noticed, for Viv noticed everything, but she kindly didn't make a big deal about the "my Sean". Her sophisticated eye took in the original inlaid mosaic floors, the minimalist smattering of heavy, sculpted chairs, made to look lush and touchable under perfectly angled spotlights. Elegant, modern, secure, with a nod to the old ways. So very, very Sean.

It had been nearly three days since she'd seen him. The longest amount of time apart since they'd met.

They'd messaged back and forth dozens of times. She'd sent him a picture of the sad little coffee she'd made in her room. Decaf now, alas. He'd sent her a photo of the mosaic on the floor of a fancy restaurant in which he was meeting a client.

She'd sent him a picture of Frank, labelled "Cheese!" Frank had not smiled at all. Sean had sent her a drawing of Elwood another client's four-year-old daughter had made for him in bright purple crayon. The caption, "Now this is art."

That one had cut. Deep. That he found that charming. That a little girl liked him enough to have made him a picture.

"What do you think?" she asked, her voice a little high.

Viv turned to Aubrey, silver brows raised. "I never saw you as the type who needed a beard, my dear."

"Sorry?"

"Am I to be a distraction for your young man when you tell him your news?"

"No! I just—" She lost her nerve pretty fast. And leant her head on Viv's shoulder. "No. But you can hold me upright till then."

Viv patted her hand. "Even the strongest of us are not strong all the time. There is no light without dark. No power without vulnerability. No—"

"Aubrey!" Enzo's voice called from down the way. "*Bella ragazza.* It has been days since you have graced my humble bistro. How are my Flora and Angelina? *Le mie belle figlie.* And how is—?"

Enzo stopped, his gaze alighting on something wondrous over Aubrey's shoulder.

Aubrey turned to find Viv walking towards her, her cheeks pink, eyes shining. She even lifted her hand to check her hair.

Frank, sensing changing strange currents in the air, stepped in.

Aubrey stilled him with a look. "It's okay. I'll vouch for the man. Give her a moment."

Frank frowned. Max panted. Enzo stopped, bowed from the waist and held out a hand. "Enzo Frenetti. At your service."

Viv took his hand. "Vivian Ascot."

Enzo smoothly tucked her hand into the held-out crook of his arm. "*Per favore, bella signore. Do you care for tiramisu? Or cassata Siciliana, panna cotta, babà, tartufo di Pizzo...?*"

They'd just eaten, yet Viv, a hand to her décolletage, said, "Surprise me."

Aubrey looked to Frank with an eyebrow raised. "Ever seen its like?" she asked.

Frank shook his head, then lumbered after his employer, her little sausage dog in tow.

Aubrey took her phone out of her backpack to check the time. To find a message from Sean. No photo this time, only a pin in a map.

She recognised the destination. It made her smile. Then her stomach lurched. Reminding her what she was walking into.

It would be a miracle if he took the news well, and she'd used up her one miracle already. She only wished they'd had more time. More time simply being them, before they were about to become something neither of them had gone into this thing prepared to be.

She sent a message to Frank to let him know she was heading off to meet Sean. She'd catch up with them later. Much later, if the look in Viv's eye was anything to go by.

Taking a quick sip of the lemon water from the bottle in her backpack, she wiped a little extra across the back of her hot neck, and set off.

* * *

Aubrey stood looking at the David.

He really was a marvel. All sinew and glorious musculature. She'd totally paint him on something one day. Maybe just his hand reaching for a door handle, looking as if it had torn through the metal.

But the urge to touch him was no longer there. Not when she'd already had the real thing.

A security guard walked by. Different from the one she'd befriended her first day in town. What was that, five weeks ago now? Six?

She gave him a smile. He gave her a nod. It was enough. She wasn't sure she had it in her to make new friends today.

She was too wired. And tired. And hot. And nauseous. And terrified to the bottoms of her sandals that Sean, for how far he'd come, would turn to stone the moment she said those life-changing words.

What if his demons were too great? His determination not to care much too entrenched? What if his feelings…? She gulped. What if his feelings simply weren't on a par with hers? Even considering his colossal heart and her busted one.

Feeling a little soft in the head, she moved to the edge of the room and leaned against the wall. Her forehead felt tight, as if it was trying to break out in a sweat.

It was hot out there today. And she'd not ambled. Her desire to see him, to hold him, to kiss him, to absorb him, greater than her fear about what came next.

"Aubrey?"

Aubrey spun, and the world kept spinning.

"Hey, stranger!" Her voice sounded odd to her ears. As if it were coming from far away.

But her joy at seeing Sean kept her upright.

Fresh from a meeting, he wore black suit pants, a pure white button-down shirt tucked in, tie tucked into the pocket, top buttons popped open, and sleeves rolled to his elbows. He looked healthy and blue-eyed and beautiful.

He had a small basket in hand and a picnic blanket under his arm. And she knew, she just knew, his plan was to set up a little spot in the middle of the floor for as long as they could before they were kicked out.

It was the single most romantic thing anyone had ever done for her.

She laughed, or at least she tried to. She no longer felt as if she had control over her mouth. Or her face. Then her vision started turning black at the edges.

She saw Sean's face, his beautiful face, come over anxious before he dropped everything and ran towards her. But only in slow motion. It was the weirdest thing.

The second last thing she noted, before the world turned black, was the wretched fear in his eyes. As if his world were crumbling before his eyes.

The last was how much she loved him for it.

Audrey woke with cold bright light shining through the backs of her eyelids. She opened them, slowly, to find herself looking at a utilitarian ceiling. No chubby cherubs. No David poster behind her bed. No chandelier.

But there was a woman in a lab coat writing on a chart, and another taking her pulse. An IV dripped into the back of her hand.

She was in a hospital. A language she couldn't catch murmuring around her. As situations went in Aubrey land, it was about as bad as it could be. The flashback to the months spent in a hospital in Copenhagen brought her out in an instant cold sweat.

"Aubrey?"

She blinked to focus on the woman in the lab coat. It was the cardiologist she'd seen the afternoon before. Her voice shook with relief as she said, "Dr Ricci."

"*Sì.* Hello, Aubrey. Do you know why you are here?" she asked.

And a brand-new panic set in. "I… I fainted. Near the David."

"I do not blame you; he is one fine specimen of man. I know, I'm a doctor." Dr Ricci smiled, then placed a hand on Aubrey's shoulder. "You are fine. Your heart is strong. The baby's heartbeat is pumping away beautifully. We need to make sure you are fit enough to walk out of here, but the signs point to it being dehydration. By the colour in your cheeks, on your shoulders, I'd suggest you were overheated. Were you out in the sun today? Walking?"

Walking fast. To get to the David. To get to Sean. *Sean.* The look on his face when she'd begun to fall. The full-blown terror. She had to let him know she was okay.

"Sean?" Aubrey tried to sit up but her head swam.

Dr Ricci pressed Aubrey back into the bed. "Stay. Rest. I'd like to keep you in here a few more hours, just for observation."

Aubrey slumped back onto the pillow and closed her eyes shut tight. Observation. That's what they'd said last time. When hours had become months.

Before panic took over, she inhaled deeply. Placed a hand over her heart, another over her belly. Checked in. Reminding herself they were both fine.

"Now," said Dr Ricci. "This Sean. He is the dashing gentleman who brought you in?"

Aubrey nodded.

"He claimed he was your friend. Or more than a friend, if I remember the nurses at reception speaking correctly. They were in quite the twitter."

"He is super hot," Aubrey managed, her head feeling a little swimmy again before she felt herself dragged under.

"Rest," Dr Ricci's voice came from a long way away. "I'll check on you again soon."

When Aubrey woke again she felt much better. The light had changed. She felt cool and clean and rested.

She opened her eyes and tipped her head to find Sean, seated upright in the chair by her bed, asleep. She wondered what he'd said or done to force his way in here. She wished she'd been awake to see it.

She watched him for a few moments, remembering the last thought she'd had, just before she'd blacked out. Knowing it hadn't been due to a lack of oxygen.

She loved this man.

She was in love with him.

He was a mile from the nice, docile guy she'd imagined she'd end up with. A man she now knew would have bored her silly.

She still wanted the same things she always had. Love. And family. And joy.

But the form it took? That wasn't something one could prescribe. Done right, it was organic and tempestuous and joyful and hard. It was a process. An awakening. It took work. And for two people to find one another at just the right time, when they were ready and raring to go on the same journey together.

She'd come on this trip with the burning desire to figure out her future. There was a strange relief in knowing it was something she'd could never have known till it happened.

She dragged herself to sitting. When the bed sheets rustled, Sean opened his eyes, and moved to her side in an instant, his hand wrapping around hers, his lips going to her forehead. She dragged her hand into his hair and held him there.

"I'm fine," she said eons later.

"I know." Sean's voice was rough. Raw. "Still, that was not fun. Seeing you collapse like that. I thought—"

"I know."

Ending up in hospital was right up there with Aubrey's worst nightmares. Seeing someone he cared about collapse was Sean's. And while he might not be in love with her, not the way she now knew she loved him, he did care.

Only now the time had come to see how much.

Aubrey let her hand fall to his chest, and said, "There's more."

He breathed in long and slow through his nose, the slight flare of his nostrils giving away the fact that he was still on edge.

"You might need to sit down for this one."

"I'd like to stay right here, if that's okay."

She nodded. Wished she'd figured out the exact right words to say this. Then in the end went with the simple, unadorned truth.

"I'm pregnant."

A shadow passed over Sean's face. "I know."

"How?" she asked, her throat tight. Her eyes darting over his face, trying to pick up any kind of sign as to what he might be thinking.

"I listened in when the doctor was talking to the nurse."

"How devious," she said.

But Sean didn't laugh. He didn't move a muscle.

"Uh oh," she said, her tone light, even as her insides twisted.

"What?" he said.

"You took a Sean moment."

"A—"

"You take a breath or blink before speaking, as if lining up your words just right before releasing them into the world. Especially when they are words you think I might not like."

This time a muscle twitched in his cheek. And she felt him pulling away from her.

No, no, no, no...

She gripped his hand tighter, using it to pull herself to sitting. "Look at me, Malone. We have to talk this through. *Sean.*"

His eyes snapped to hers and she held his gaze.

Hoping he might see the feelings in her eyes, that she was too scared to say with her words.

"I'm pregnant. With your baby. It's inside me right now. Its tiny heart beating. I think it's miraculous, but you have every right to feel shock. Or fear. Or concern. Or delight. Happiness. Celebration."

Still nothing.

She looked around for her backpack. Her phone. "I have a photo. And a video—"

Sean stepped back as he made a sound, something like a hollow laugh. Or a groan. "No."

Her hand paused on the mouth of her backpack. Her voice reed thin as she said, "No? You don't want to see?"

His hand went over his mouth. His chin, his throat. His eyes beseeched her. "Aubrey, what the hell happened?"

If only she knew what those eyes were truly asking for. Comfort? Solidarity? Absolution? Without a map, without a clue, she swallowed and played to her strengths. Said, "When a man and a woman make love—"

He cut her off with a look. Okay, so he *wasn't* after comic relief.

But right now, humour was the only thing stopping her from breaking down completely. From *begging* him to stop moving away. To tell her how he was feeling. To yell at her, or cry with her. To just hold her. To know she was scared too. And to reciprocate her joy, her love. For ever, if he could. That would be fabulous.

"You said…" he began. "You told me you couldn't."

"I was told it would be nearby impossible. Clearly a huge amount of hanky-panky helps beat the odds."

There. Finally! A flicker of heat. Of understanding that she was doing her best here.

He *knew* her. He knew this was her way. If he could bend, just a little, rather than fall back on the stoic inability to let people in that had been his benchmark before she came along, they might find a way through this.

But then he rubbed his eyes and wiped all evidence of a connection away. "Look. Can you be serious, just for a second? Tell me, convince me, that all this has not put you in danger. Your heart."

A strange haze came over her then, some ancient mother instinct. *"All this?* If by that you mean the peanut growing inside of me—"

His eyes flared then. As if he'd been readying for the fight. Itching for it. To step back behind the ramparts, back inside his comfort zone. A place she didn't belong.

"If the doctors thought it was nearby impossible, can your body even handle this?"

"My cardiologist and OB/GYN have assured me everything looks as it should. No evidence of side effects from my meds. I stopped them immediately, which is fine as their levels were as near to a placebo as it was possible to get."

She hoped to see a measure of relief. Instead, even more barricades came crashing down.

"You've known about this long enough to see doctors? Plural?"

Aubrey swallowed, though it felt more like a gulp. "Not that long. It all happened so fast. The discovery. The check-ups. I didn't want to concern you until I knew it was real. That it was possible. That it was all okay."

"All okay," he repeated, his tone incredulous, as if it was anything but.

Feeling too tender to control herself, she shot back, "As for the rest, how it affects me as the months go on, I guess the only answer is *We'll see.*"

It was the truth, but she'd chosen not to soften it. She'd wanted the reaction, wanted to shake him out of his stillness. The look he shot her was hard, hot, and dismayed. But dammit, *she* was scared too.

"I don't want your pity, Malone."

"I don't pity you. I'm…in shock. And concerned. And in a position I never planned to put myself in."

She was getting that. "This is all very new to me too, okay? I'm still trying to come to terms with it myself. I'm pregnant. After having been told it was not on the cards. You know how devastated I was. Yet here I am, with what might be my only chance to do this. But I believe, truly, it doesn't have to change anything between us. Un-less... Unless we want it to."

"Aubrey," he said, rearing back. "You can't be serious."

Wow. Like a dagger to the chest. He couldn't have aimed more squarely if he'd tried.

"I am. I am serious. Can you honestly say, when we first met, that you had a single clue that the past few weeks were even possible?"

Something flickered behind his eyes then.

"No? Me neither. Yet it's been the time of my life. And not because of some fancy hotel, or a whole lot of amazing art. But because I met you."

Her voice broke at the last. Emotion uncoiling inside her till she could no longer control it.

But while she could feel his energy, the force of it, shaking to be set free, he remained unflinch-ing in his determination not to yield.

"I just... I don't get it, Malone. Are you wait-ing for permission?"

"For what?"

"To love me!" she cried, her arms out wide.

The room was so quiet after, her words seemed to catch on the air-conditioning current and bounce about the room.

Aubrey felt tears streaming down her face and she swiped them away with a hard hand to each cheek. Then she felt the hospital gown fall off her shoulder. She yanked it back into place, feeling horribly exposed. "I didn't… I didn't mean that. I just meant… You know what. It doesn't matter—"

Sean spoke, his voice so husky she missed it.

"Sorry? What was that?"

His jaw worked as he looked at the ceiling. "I said, I can't."

"Can't…? Oh."

He couldn't *love her*.

Not enough, anyway. Not enough to leap. To take what they had and turn it into something more. Bigger. Whole. A family. For ever.

Tears still streaming down her face, she looked down at the sheet pooled at her waist. "I think I'd like you to leave."

"Not happening. I'm staying till they let you go."

"Malone, you're killing me here."

"You think this isn't hurting me too? I've been sitting here for hours, since I heard the news. After seeing you faint. Watching you lie there. Knowing that all that was keeping you alive was your damaged heart. You, and the baby. My baby."

He looked off into the distance, a hand rubbing over his mouth as he spoke. Aubrey bit her lip.

"I too imagined," he went on, "when I was younger, that one day I'd meet a girl, fall in love, have kids. But it was a concept. A determination that when it happened I'd do it differently from my own parents. I'd be gentler. Kinder. I'd choose to prioritise my kids. I'd love them so hard they never ever doubted me.

"Watching you lie there in that bed, a drip in your hand, suddenly I was my parents. With this tiny helpless creature in my care." As if he'd sensed her intake of breath, her readying to speak, he cut her off. "And no, by that I did not mean you."

"Right. Sorry. Go on."

"What if something happened? What if you lost it? What if I—?"

Aubrey held her breath, absolutely sure he'd been about to say *What if I lost you?*

"My parents…" He stopped. Swallowed. "My parents raised us, brought us to adulthood, only to lose Carly. And then… And then I left. I left and they lost me too."

If Aubrey weren't attached to a drip and feeling as if she'd been hit by a truck, she'd have leapt out of her bed and into his arms, and held him tight till he held her right on back.

Instead, she had to watch as his eyes finally met hers again. Tortured. And apologetic. Decided.

"I may look like a living breathing human person, but I'm not, Aubrey. Not in the way you need. The way you deserve. The way a child—"

Aubrey's heart twisted and squeezed, riddled with her own pain. And his. "Malone, stop," she finally managed. "What happened with your sister, it wasn't your fault."

He threw his hands in the air and began to pace. "I promised I'd take her in hand. That I'd help her get her head sorted. And I failed. Of course it was my fault."

"It wasn't your fault."

The small private room seemed to shrink the more he paced. "I let myself become distracted. And she spiralled so fast. It broke all of us. And we couldn't... No matter how much we wanted it, we couldn't put each other back together again. I can't go through that again. I won't."

He was shouting now.

A nurse popped her head in the door.

Aubrey held up a hand, shook her head.

The nurse took a look at Sean and melted away.

Aubrey looked to the ceiling. She was good with words. Maybe even better than she was with a pencil. How was she messing this up so badly?

"I'm going to say this one more time. It wasn't your fault. You are that good a man, Malone. You've provided work, and respite, and opportunity, and comfort, and shelter, and friendship, and kindness to so many people in your sphere all while convincing yourself you were alone. You are a living, breathing human person, Malone, the livingest, breathingest I've ever known. With a big strong heart. Big enough for the both of us, if you'll just let it do its thing. No matter what the voices in your head are telling you."

They looked at one another across the room, both breathing heavily. At an impasse. Both at a loss as to what to do next. What else was there to say? To convince the other that they were right.

Then Sean pulled himself upright and she saw the architect, the boss, the good son, the island, and she braced herself for whatever might come next.

"I will contribute," he said. "Time, money. Whatever the baby needs."

Ready for it, still she flinched at the finality in his voice. "Contribute. Well, that sounds like fun."

"Fun? You think that's what we're arguing about here? How much fun we can make this… this…"

Aubrey's entire body cooled by a good degree. "This what? Disaster? This tragedy? It's a baby, Sean. A tiny cluster of cells hanging on dearly to life. That hustle, that desire to *live*, despite all the walls my body had put in its way, I respect the hell out of this kid of ours already. Malone—"

He cut her off. "It is a miracle. Life is a miracle. The fact that any of us are here, the things we survive, is utterly humbling. Yet, you make jokes, Aubrey. And I get that's your way of dealing with some pretty heavy stuff in your life. But you need to respect that my way of dealing is to retreat and collect my head. Whether that takes a moment, or years."

He was trying to appear as if he knew what he wanted, but he seemed so lost. She bit her lip and tried to wait him out. But, as was her way, she leapt. "Malone—"

"Enough." When his eyes met hers they were burning. Ferocious. Full. "I suggest you do the same. Take some time to really think. Because right now, I can't see how it would work. Especially when you still struggle to call me by my name."

Aubrey gaped. Readying to defend herself. Until she realised she had no defence. He was utterly, one hundred per cent, in the right.

She called him Malone as if it was cute. Banter. She was the one who'd made all the noise about them being finite.

We're friends. A summer fling. Let's promise to be light and easy. Till the day I decide to walk away.

She'd told herself she was doing him a favour. Giving him the illusion of space. When the truth was, she was the one who'd needed it. Used it to self-protect. To remain one step removed from true intimacy. From heartache. From loss.

On her next breath out she deflated. Completely. Falling back onto the bed, she pulled the sheets up to her chin. Feeling as if she could sleep for a hundred years.

"Aubrey," he said, his voice throaty, sounding as wrung out as she felt.

"Mm hmm."

"Will you stay? In Florence? I hope you do. The hospitals here are top-notch."

"Glad to hear it."

"Or will you go home? I need to know how to stay in touch."

Her subconscious screamed, *You are my home, you big lug!* But she closed her eyes so he wouldn't see it. She already felt foolish enough.

"Not yet sure," she said. She'd held onto a tiny thread of hope that he might have made the decision easy. "I might yet continue on with the trip. The doctors I saw— Viv has me hooked up with the best across Europe. Just in case. I put my foot down at taking the Lear jet... Oh, God! I was meant to check in with her. She has no idea I'm here."

"How can I contact her for you?"

"Her number is in my phone. And last I saw her she was with Enzo."

"Enzo?" he said, his voice barely curious, as if all the colour had leeched out. "Leave it to me. Let me do this for you."

This. Not love her. Not be with her. Not raise their baby together. Make a phone call.

She was too exhausted to fight it any more. She opened her eyes and found his. "So much for our deal. Where I was the one who got to walk away. To catch my foot on a sheet and make a right ruckus."

The humour was weak, but by that point it was all she had left.

"I'm not walking away from you, Aubrey. Or the baby. But us… It needs to stop here. Before things get confused." He came back to her then, took her hand, lifted her palm to his lips and kissed her. "I never want to regret you, Aubrey."

"I never want to regret you either," she said. Then, in a last-ditch effort at self-protection, added, "Malone."

He sniffed out a laugh, then let her go and walked to the door. He turned and asked, one last time, "Are you sure you're okay?"

"Not so much," she said, the first truly honest moment of her day. "But I will be. And so will you, Sean. I promise, so will you."

CHAPTER TEN

BAGS PACKED, AUBREY took one last look around her fancy hotel room, making sure she hadn't left anything behind.

Anything, that was, apart from her heart. Busted as it was, she'd miss it. It had served her well. It had led her to Sean, after all. The man who'd kick-started her dreams again. Dreams that weren't to be.

In their place, international co-parenting.

They'd find a way to make it work. Even while it would ache, seeing him. Unable to hold him. To kiss him. To lean into him when tired. To fall apart in seconds when he did that thing with his pinkie finger.

Till then…she'd decided it was best to go home.

Her parents would be so excited. Another grandchild in the mix.

Though they'd protest, she was doing this on her own. She'd find a cute little cottage with a yard. Room for a paddling pool. And maybe even a dog. A little smaller than Elwood. A lot more smarts.

Her life hadn't ended when her heart had stopped. It had been given a new start.

And she was still determined to follow her curiosity and see where it led.

But first, sitting on the edge of her bed, she nibbled on a cracker, sipped a little warm water, had a quick suck on a lemon to make sure she didn't throw up, then returned the call she'd missed the day before.

The first step towards filling in the rest of her world on what her new normal was about to become.

Daisy answered first. "Morning, sunshine!"

Who'd stolen Daisy and put this Daisy-shaped person in her place? "You're chipper."

"Yeah, I am!"

Jessica popped up. This time *she* was yawning. "We really need to line up our chat times better. Who called? Aubrey? Everything wonderful and brilliant wherever in the world you are today?"

"Still Florence."

"Huh, thought you'd have seen half of Italy by now."

"I'm actually leaving today."

"Perfect timing!" That was Daisy. "Guess what? We're doing a surprise gig in Copenhagen! The boys and I. An anniversary gig, though on a much smaller scale. Jay owns this club there. It's brilliant, like an old-fashioned speakeasy. And we're going to make a surprise appearance. It's three days from now and I want you guys to come."

A tiny spark lit inside the wasteland that was Aubrey's enthusiasm, as if the peanut were cheering, *Yes! Travel! I love to travel! Let's do it.*

"And bring Sean! I promise not to drool on him. And I'll make Jay promise the same. When he found out you guys were friends, he turned into a blushing schoolgirl. Apparently, Malone's chairs are like rock-star porn."

Aubrey shook her head, infinitesimally. It was too much. The talk of drool. And Sean's beautiful chairs. And, well, porn.

Jessica, being Jessica, noticed. "Aubs? You okay?"

"What? No. I'm fine. But it'll just be me."

"No hot wood guy?"

"No hot wood guy," she parroted back, her voice sounding clownish. She cleared her throat, settled herself down. And said, "Just me. Which is fine, because I have so much I want to catch you guys up on! But I'll save it till in person. Much better that way."

Besides, she needed to get off the phone. Her throat felt as if it was closing up. And the backs of her eyes were burning.

"No," said Daisy. "You don't look right. Tell us now."

Aubrey blinked and a single tear fell down her cheek. And that opened the floodgates. She told her girls everything. Well, everything bar Sean's magical pinky-finger move. That she saved just for her.

"A baby," said Jessica, her eyes round. And full of wonder. "Oh, Aubrey. That's wonderful. And when you thought it wouldn't be possible."

While Daisy stared down the phone as if she

wished she could jump through the thing and hold Aubrey close.

"Daisy?" Aubrey said. "You okay?"

"What? Yes. I'm assuming Sean's the father?"

"Of course he's the father. Jeez!"

"I'm in London right now but I can get to you in a matter of hours. You know, if you need me to have a word."

"With Sean?" Aubrey felt laughter unexpectedly bubble into her throat. "No! He's promised to 'contribute'. And I fully believe him. He just… he just doesn't want me as part of the bargain."

The girls all let that sit, like a dark foggy cloud making it hard to breathe.

"How can that be? We saw the way he looked at you on the phone that day, when he so kindly greeted us in nothing but a towel."

Aubrey rolled onto her back, holding the phone above her face. A complete glutton for punishment, she asked, "And how was that?"

"Like he couldn't believe his luck," Jessica said.

Aubrey let the phone fall to her chest for a moment, while she collected herself.

"You're in love with him, aren't you?" Daisy's voice hummed.

Aubrey lifted the phone, and nodded.

"But I'm guessing, by the way things turned out, you never said so."

"Not in so many words. More like I made him promise to keep things light and easy and fun. I rarely called him by his first name. And any time things became serious, I cracked a joke."

"That's our girl," Jessica murmured.

"Look," said Daisy, glancing over her shoulder, "I really have to go. We're in final rehearsal for the gig before we fly out tonight. Tell me you'll be there."

"I'll be there," Aubrey promised. "So long as you have crackers and lemons on hand so I don't hurl."

"Done. I've just sent all the details. Time. Date. Name on the door. All you have to do for me is be far less maudlin."

"Done. A good sixty…sixty-five per cent less."

"Good girl. Jess?" Daisy asked.

"Yes! I'm in. I'll get someone to cover me at work for a few days. This is going to be brilliant. We can all finally debrief about the crazy last few months in person. And do the ring test on Aubrey to see if it's a girl or a boy. All good things."

When the girls looked to her, in the hopes of having cheered her up, Aubrey forced a smile. "First thing on the agenda? Viv's new boyfriend."

"What?" the girls said in unison, before Aubrey hung up.

She watched her friends disappear from their squares, one after the other. Then stared at the little pop-up that came up at the end of the call.

If you love this app, please review! Click here to rewatch.

After a beat, Aubrey clicked. Her heart racing, just a little, when she saw all her video chats had been saved into a folder.

Thumb racing now, she scrolled and scrolled and...there!

Her third morning in Florence. The conversation from Sean's bed.

She fast forwarded, through Daisy's frowns and Jessica's sighs, until...

She paused on a shot when Sean had walked into the room. The moment she knew he was coming up behind her.

She looked so happy. And relaxed. As if she had not a care in the world. When before meeting Sean, she'd been a right mess.

Whereas he...

Attempting to look beyond the towel slung low around his hips, the super muscles and tanned skin, his hair falling over his eye, she saw the smile. Honest. Sensual. And a little surprised. As if he didn't know what he was in for, but it was too late now. He was already on board.

She played it again, and paused on the moment his eyes met hers.

Her heart clutched. She rested a hand on her chest. And remembered back to how she'd felt in that moment. To think how much deeper her feelings now went. Now that she knew him. Now that she'd seen how he treated others. Now she knew how hard he was on himself.

Yet, in the hospital room, she'd pushed for an answer. Knowing he didn't respond to that kind of pressure. When what she ought to have done was be there. Beside him. Supporting him. Holding him. Giving him the chance to catch up to her much faster schedule in his own time. Then, when he came out of his cave, she'd be there. Loving him.

But it was done now. Over. She couldn't wait for ever. Not only because she'd finally given the hotel her notice of departure. But because she wasn't making decisions for only herself any more.

But she had an hour. Maybe a little more before she had to hand in her key.

And there was one more thing she had to do before she left.

Sean would have liked nothing more than to hole up in his workshop, alone, with a hunk of wood and a piece of sandpaper, for the next few months.

It used to soothe him when he was a kid. Finding some place quiet in his head to turn over his thoughts. Turning the rough to smooth. The rugged into something that made sense.

Only now there were people everywhere he looked. People he'd been stupid enough to hire.

He could feel Flora's angry gaze burning between his shoulder blades. Even Angelina couldn't look him in the eyes. Only Hans had said good morning, but likely because—hailing from a tiny village in Germany—he spoke little English and less Italian, so had no clue what was going on.

Sean had tried whacking on a set of head-phones, pumping up the Puccini, grabbing a heavy-duty chisel and just hacking at a plank of Baltic pine in the hopes of finding inspiration.

Or a way through the heavy fugue that had draped over him ever since leaving Aubrey at the hospital. He was beginning to think that fugue might linger. That it might have a terribly long half-life. Because Aubrey had been an extinction event. She'd crashed into his life like a meteor. And when the first dust cleared, the landscape was not even close to recognisable.

Problem was, he was having a hard time re-membering why that was a bad thing.

Ben cast a shadow over him, waited till he made eye contact, and asked, "How long you gonna keep that up, boss? Till you chisel that stump into a toothpick?"

Wishing for the good old days when they'd all been scared of him, Sean grabbed his laptop, left Elwood at the villa, and headed into town. He'd do some admin in the quiet privacy of the showroom.

In Via Alighieri, key in hand, he turned as Gia appeared in the doorway of her leather shop, murmuring, "Keep walking, Malone. Just keep walking."

But it was too late.

"Gian!" Enzo called, descending from his bis-

tro, hands wringing a tea towel. "What is this I hear about our Aubrey? She is gone?"

Sean hung his head, breathed deep. He had a splitting headache, his ears felt as if they were full of cotton wool and he had some kind of constriction in his chest that just wouldn't ease no matter what he ate. He didn't want to play these games today.

But Enzo was a kind man, with a good heart, and didn't deserve his bad mood. He regrouped. Took a Sean moment, as Aubrey would call it. If she were here. At his back.

"So you're Aubrey's Sean; the one who called me the other day."

Sean turned to find a woman he'd never met—posh accent, expensive clothes—and something twigged. "Vivian Ascot."

"I am she. Where's my girl?"

Aubrey was pregnant. Off her medication. Fragile. And frustrated. And disappointed in him. And yet she was okay. Always would be.

While he… He already missed her with an ache he couldn't contain.

"Mr Malone?" Vivian Ascot chastised, using the voice that had built a business empire.

Sean's hand gripped his keys. Then he breathed out hard. "She's on her way to Copenhagen to catch up with her friends. Your friends. Jess and Daisy? She sent me a message this morning."

They were keeping in touch, as promised. It was all very civilised.

"Thank you."

Sean nodded, and moved inside, locking the door behind him.

Civilised. How had it come to that? From the very moment they'd met their relationship had been built on friction. His obstinate grip on the status quo. Her determined need for change. She was dauntless. Presumptuous. Meddlesome. And she'd won out, more often than not.

Except this last time. This time he'd won. Though it sure didn't feel like any kind of victory he'd care to choose.

Sean took a step, his foot slipping on a piece of paper on the floor.

He recognised the slanting script on the front as Aubrey's hand.

She'd taken to leaving notes around his workshop. On his bed. In the fridge—*'When life shuts a door...open it. It's a door—that's how they work'* and *'Always trust people who like big butts—they cannot lie'*—in case he ever wanted a tattoo.

It took him a moment longer to notice it wasn't a note, but an envelope. With only one word written on the front. His name.

Not Malone.

Sean.

His lungs tightened. He breathed through it. Told himself not to read into it.

He'd been reading into her expressions, her movements, her attention, her smiles, for weeks.

Looking for signs that she might be feeling as he did. Falling deeper and deeper with each passing day. Each sublime night.

But he'd never been able to feel any assurance that she was all in. How could she be? She'd come to Florence to suck the marrow out of life; he'd come to Florence to hide.

Still, there had been moments when he'd seen past her humour, to a glimpse of something deeper. Some flash of desire. A wash of affection. A moment of true, rare connection in which he saw a vision of what a future, together, might look like.

Then she'd say, "Fun! Light! Easy! Casual!" And she'd call him Malone.

So he'd held back. Kept his feelings in check. Until he'd walked into the Galleria to see her faint. Her face deathly pale. Her eyes rolling back in her head.

He'd never run so fast, getting to her just before she hit the floor.

The feel of her in his arms—limp, a rag doll— had been the single most terrifying moment of his life. His shout for the guard to call for an ambulance must have made every statue in that place flinch.

Hearing the doctors say that she was okay— that it was heat, not her heart, that had knocked her out—had made his legs near give way with relief. Promises had tripped over themselves in the back of his head. Promises to tell her how he felt the moment she woke up.

That he adored her, and that she had saved him, and that while he wanted her to travel, to see the world, he wanted her to know she could always come home to him.

And then to find out she was pregnant...

He knew it was possible to breeze through pregnancy. But he also knew a child could wreak havoc on even the healthiest body. His own mother had pulled that one out of the bag whenever Carly was acting ungrateful. That she'd nearly died on the table having her.

Their mother had wondered, out loud, just the once, in a rare moment of frailty, if that pressure was why Carly acted the way she did. Each of them burdened with their share of guilt.

When in the end, the truth was far more simple. Carly was an addict. She made many bad choices. One of which had ended her life.

Choices. Choices were hard enough for someone whose head was clear.

Love me! Aubrey had cried, while curled up on the hospital bed.

Seeing her in the hospital gown, so big it fell off her shoulder, her face pale, her eyes scared, he'd taken too long a moment and the moment had been lost. Any other day, if she'd looked him in the eye and said, *Love me,* he might have made the better choice. To grab her, hold her close and say, *Always*.

Sean looked down at the envelope in his hands. How long had it been there? Days? Weeks?

He couldn't open it. Not now when he still felt so raw. He went to put the envelope onto the bench but at the last second said, "Screw it," and tore the edge open.

What he found inside was no joke at all.

The very first thing he saw was a photograph. Black and white. A speckled grey mass, with a dark splodge in the middle.

A sonogram. Aubrey's name in one corner, Baby Malone written in the other. And in the centre, a peanut. Clear as day.

Sean moved to sit on one of the stools by the bench.

Why had she sent this to him? Was it a parting gift? Or a last-ditch plea?

Look what we did.
Look what we made.
Love me.

Aubrey never had been afraid to play dirty.

Adrenaline bucketing through him, Sean opened up the other papers inside the envelope. Stationery from her hotel. Each piece of paper branded with a sketch.

A hand holding a lathe. A finger—short nails, scarred—running across a pair of closed lips. A pair of eyes, looking directly at the artist. His eyes. His hands. His lips. His father's nose. His mother's dark hair. And Carly's stubborn jaw. A dozen drawings. Each with the fluidity he'd seen in her that first day. But it was the detail that had his lungs emptying in a rush. The study.

The *intimacy*.

He went back through them till he found the eyes.

He'd avoided mirrors for years; the pain he'd see in his face, the guilt, only piling on. But in the drawing, his eyes were clear. Laughing. Charmed. Was this how he looked when Aubrey was in the room? If so, there was no way she didn't know his feelings for her.

But for all her joy, her spirit, she'd been through the wringer too. Her faith in her own happiness was shaken. She might not trust all the good she saw. She'd needed to be told.

All people needed to be told. To hear the words. I want you. I can't live without you.

I forgive you.

Gathering the scattered papers in one hand, Sean dialled her number with the other, then tucked his phone beneath his chin. But it rang out. She was probably already on the plane to Copenhagen.

He hung up. Locked up.

Striding down the street, he called another number. His own.

"Sì," said Flora, the only one who ever answered the landline.

"Hey, it's me. Can you look after Elwood for a few days?"

"Of course. So long as it means I can stay here. And have full use of the bar. Papa has a new girlfriend, some rich English lady, and I can't watch. Do I need to guess where it is you might be going?"

"Yeah," he said, surprising himself. "I think maybe you do."

A little over thirty-six hours later, Sean's driver pulled up outside a Melbourne building covered in scaffolding. A man in a suit, and a black and white striped tie, president of the football club and old family friend, barrelled his way towards him the moment he got out of the car.

"Sean! So good to see you my boy," said George. "When I got your message, I was thrilled. Can't express how much. No luggage?"

"Not staying long."

George nodded. "Fair enough. Come on in so I can show you the space."

Sean followed. Taking a moment to breathe in his surroundings.

Midwinter and the weather in Melbourne was as per usual: chilly, with sunshine beaming through the grey clouds. It hadn't been the weather that had kept him away.

"He here?" Sean asked.

George looked over his shoulder, didn't have to ask who.

"He's inside. I didn't tell him you were coming.

That was how you wanted it, right? I want you to know, it doesn't feel good not telling your mother."

"She knows. I went by home to see her first." Sean scratched the edge of his nose. "Was worried she might keel over from the surprise."

"And did she?"

"She took it well."

Better than well. Sean's mother had dragged him into her arms and not let go for a good five minutes. After which she'd made him a coffee, forced him to eat cake the cook had made, and held his hand tightly as he'd given her a rundown of the past five years of his life.

When he'd asked after her, she'd just shaken her head. Sniffed loudly. Looked at him fiercely. And said, "None of that matters. It all begins again from here."

And he'd believed her. Believed that they could overcome the mistakes they'd made in turning away from one another and not in. He'd seen it happen. A life beginning anew. Hinging on a single moment. Nothing that came after ever the same as what had gone before.

He'd not planned on telling her about Aubrey, but as if he'd needed to tell someone, to say the words out loud, it had all spilled out. How they'd met. How she'd infiltrated his life. How she'd shifted his perceptions of everything. From time to forgiveness. To the limits he'd put on his life. His capacity to feel joy. To feel at all.

When he'd got to the ending, the ending as things stood now, a child, her grandchild, his mother had swallowed hard, a torrid mix of happiness and sadness behind her eyes. Then she'd hugged him hard, told him she was sure he would find a way to make things work out for the best. That it was his gift. And his burden. But if she had a say, she'd very much like to meet this young woman one day soon.

And Sean knew, more than he'd ever known anything his entire life, that if he had a say, he'd make that happen.

"Well," said George, tears welling, throat clearing. "Then you've made my day, boy. My year. Don't much care if you refuse to take my commission now. Actually, I do care. Would put us on the map, culturally speaking, so do consider it rightly."

The doors to the front of the building whispered open, a pair of famous footballers in black and white tracksuits shouldering their way past with polite nods.

And inside, standing by the front desk, in a hard hat and tweed jacket, Sean's father.

"Brian," Sean called. But his voice barely travelled past the tightness in his throat. He cleared it, took a breath, and called, "Dad."

He saw his father still. Breathe out.

And turn.

CHAPTER ELEVEN

AUBREY FELT AS if she was in a Daisy and Jessica sandwich, the girls hugged her so hard.

"Don't squish the baby," she managed between her smushed lips.

The girls both sprang away as if they'd been electrified.

"Kidding. Peanut is about the size of a raspberry right now."

Thinking about Peanut made her think of Sean. Which meant she was thinking about him a thousand times a day. The fact that he was no longer in her days. Or her nights. The wondering if he'd found her envelope. If it had sparked any kind of revelation. Or even if he was simply somewhere in the world thinking about her too.

She shook it off. She was with her best friends in the world. And if that didn't go some ways to cheering her up, nothing would. "Viv—in a bid to be actual godmother not merely fairy godmother—had me checked out by the best and brightest and so far so good."

Jessica slid a hand around her arm and leant her head on her shoulder. "Viv's not going to be the only godmother, right?"

"Of course not. Daisy too."

Jessica laughingly slapped her on the arm. Then

swiped away a tear. "Sorry. It's all a little emotional. This has just been the best summer of my life. And finishing it up by seeing you guys…"

They fell into another group hug, only this time Jessica was in the middle.

To think they'd managed to build such a strong friendship from the other side of the world. International friendship. Now international parenting. It was a whole new world out there!

"Now what's this about Viv? And some new man in her life? So much to discuss," said Daisy, checking the time on her phone, "none of which you are allowed to even hint at without me. But I really have to head backstage."

Daisy dashed away.

While Aubrey took her chance to hitch the deep neckline of her fabulous black, bare-shouldered, all-in-one jumpsuit. It looked as if she were wearing a push-up bra when really she wore none at all. Ah, pregnancy. On that score, she snaffled a cracker from her backpack.

"Aubs?" said Jessica, a funny note in her voice.

Aubrey wiped cracker crumbs from her lips. "Mmm?"

"That dashing man over there, the one looking at you like he wants to kiss you and throttle you at the same time, is that who I think it is?"

Aubrey glanced over her shoulder. Took her half a second to spot him amidst the seething crowd. That dark swishy hair, the cool mien, those ridiculous blue eyes.

"Malone," she said on a sigh. He was so beautiful he practically glowed.

"I don't know about glowing," said Jessica, "but he is very handsome."

"Did I say that out loud?"

"Sure did. I'll leave you to it, shall I? Now where is my silver fox?"

Jessica faded into the crowd, leaving Aubrey feeling as if her feet were nailed to the ground.

Sean. Sean was here. Not holed up in his cave, licking his wounds. But out in the world. At a club, no less. And he was walking her way. Looking dark and broody and focussed and *fine*.

Once he was near enough to touch, he said, "Trusedale."

Aubrey went with, "Hello, *Sean*."

And, oh, the way his deep dark eyes lit up when she said his name.

Had it always been that easy? Yes, she thought, it really had. Which was why she'd struggled to go there. For all her determination to experience the heck out of life, Sean Malone had always been more than she knew what to do with.

Aubrey felt bumps from the left, and the right. But only vaguely. Every cell was stretching towards the man before her. There was more than shadow bristling his hard jaw. Smudges beneath his perfect blue eyes. He looked as if he hadn't slept in days.

Only one reason she could think of why he looked so messed up.

He missed her.

She took a moment, a Sean moment, to let that settle. To absorb it. And to let herself believe it. A sense of free fall had her catching her breath, before she trusted it, trusted herself, and let her heart flutter and flap and glide. And soar. Till it angled its way back to him.

"Fancy meeting you here," she said.

His gaze, shadowed in the low light, played over her face. Drinking her in as if he'd stumbled out of the desert and she were a pina colada. Or, you know, a glass of water. Either or.

"I'm a fan of the band, you know," he said.

Aubrey baulked. For a fraction of a second.

"Mocking," he said, his face slowly creasing into a grin. All flashing white teeth and eye crinkles and her heart filled so fast it nearly burst.

Only her heart didn't burst. It held strong. And true. Ready to take him on. For good. If he'd stop fighting it and let her.

The music changed, the dance floor filling fast. Aubrey was bumped again, and this time she used it as an excuse to step closer, her hand landing on Sean's chest. His arm slid around her waist, pulling her close. And they began to sway.

"I've been thinking," he said.

"First time for everything." *Really? With the jokes? Not now, you goof!*

Sean smiled down at her, his gaze hot. Hungry. "I've been considering your request."

"My request."

"To love you."

"Oh," she said on an outshot of breath.

That level of assertiveness was usually her move. It was quite the thing being on the receiving end.

Then his knee slid between hers as he turned her. And there it stayed. Till they were plastered up against one another. As close as two people could get with their clothes on.

"Here's the thing," he said, his voice clear. Calm. As if he'd come out the other end of a really big Sean moment. Ready.

While she trembled all over.

"When you made your request—for me to love you—"

"Yep. Got it."

"I need you to understand that kind of thing has never been a part of my vocabulary. I grew up in a home that was the epitome of sang-froid. We learnt young to distil our emotion. Keep it locked down tight. Use that pressure as fuel to succeed. Even after we all learned how destructive bottling it all up could be, I remained good at it. It was all I knew."

Someone walked past with glasses of beer overhead and Sean deftly moved Aubrey out of the way. Protecting. Always protecting. If she was lucky, he'd never stop.

Aubrey slid a hand into the back of Sean's hair, the slippery strands scraping through her fingers. And his gaze came back to her. Those stunning Le Mans blue eyes that she loved so very much.

"Talk to me," she said.

"So demanding," he said, pressing against her, all hard heat and promise.

She might even have swooned. Just a little. But still managed to quip, "It's part of my charm."

"That it is. So, where was I?"

"Poetically tragic hot guy, bottled emotions."

"Right," he said, clicking his fingers. "Could have had *that* as a tattoo. Until I met you."

His eyes found hers. His gaze tender. And steady. "Everything changed that day, Aubrey. Everything."

"For the better, I hope."

A smile. A dimple. A flutter in her heart.

"Better than better. My staff are happier. Walking down Via Alighieri is now like walking into a fair. Even Elwood is more spry. Though any time he hears my footsteps now only to find you're not with me, he snuffles and goes back to sleep. My whole world is not what it was. My whole world," he said once more, brushing a stray strand of hair from her cheek.

"Sean," she said, her voice cracking.

"Ask me again, Aubrey," he said, his voice deep, rough, intimate. "Ask me again to love you."

The words felt so big, her throat so full. If she said it, her life would never be the same again.

Aubrey ran a hand over his collar, untucking it from where it was endearingly hooked over on itself. Then, her voice steady, she said, "Love me, Sean Malone."

"Done."

And then he kissed her. Right there in the middle of the dance floor. It was lush and hot and delicious. It was sweet and tender and full of longing.

She loved this man with her whole entire heart. Every bit of gristle. Every life-affirming pump.

It occurred to her, in the haze of his kiss, that she hadn't told him so.

Aubrey pulled back so fast they stumbled. Sean righted the ship, which was his way.

"I love you, Sean. I love you. I'm in love with you and have been for such a long time. Possibly even for ever. And it has nothing to do with the peanut you put inside of me. Though I do love you for that too. Our feisty little miracle."

Sean moved away, just enough to look down between them.

"Are you checking out my cleavage?"

"What?"

"Look," she said, puffed out her chest. "They're bigger already. One of the benefits of pregnancy. You're welcome."

His gaze, on her eyes, was indulgent. But heated. "I was preparing to say a private hello to the peanut."

"Right. Proceed."

Hand on her hip, Sean looked down once more and said, "Hello, Peanut. I love your mother. Just want you to know that right up front. I promise to protect her, and hear her, and lean on her, and never ask if she's okay for as long as she'll let me. I saw your picture the other day. And while you're a funny-looking kid, I'm smitten with you already too."

Aubrey laughed. And hiccupped as tears filled the back of her throat.

"You two," he said, his voice dropping as he moved to look down her top, past her heart tattoo, past her scar to the new cleavage below, "I'll talk to later."

Then he pulled her back in. And they swayed. No words. Just love. Aubrey could not remember ever feeling this wonderful. As if her blood were pure champagne.

She looked up at him, because she couldn't not. "You, Sean Malone, really are the gin to my tonic. Do you think maybe that is the tattoo meant for you?"

"I'm not getting a tattoo."

"Come on! Was everything you just said for nought?"

"Not everything," he said, laying a kiss on top

of her head as they moved to the music. "For you, I am willing to try new things. Like barbecue."

"Turns out I prefer pasta."

"I can keep the workshop going. Promote Flora to project manager. Hire more cabinet makers. Then you and I can base ourselves in Sydney. I know how important your family is to you."

Aubrey's heart clutched. This man! "Or we could move to Melbourne. It doesn't suck there. It would give you the chance to reconnect with your family."

"I went home."

"You what?"

"A couple of days ago. I caught up with my mum. And my dad. I took the commission."

Aubrey hit him on the chest with a balled-up fist. "Oh, you good and wonderful man."

He caught her fist in his hand. Kissed her on the small flower ring she'd bought on the Ponte Vecchio. Unwrapped the fingers. Held them as he placed them over his heart. His glorious beast of a heart.

"Thing is, though, I love Florence," said Aubrey. "It might, in fact, be the most beautiful city on the entire planet. There are so many back streets I've yet to explore. Then there's the fact that I still haven't touched the David. Working up to that might take some planning. Might take some time. So I suggest we start there and see how we go."

"Florence it is. What about—?"

"Do we have to decide all of this tonight?"

"No, but—"

Aubrey kissed him to stop him talking.

It was the only way.

Like a hazy hum in the back of her head, Aubrey heard the crowd go wild as Daisy and Jay and the rest of Dept 135 burst onto the stage.

But Aubrey and Sean kept swaying. Kissing. Planning. Dreaming.

Three hearts, beating in perfect sync.

EPILOGUE

I'VE NEVER BEEN a fan of summer, preferring to follow more temperate climes as I travel the globe.

But this steaming hot summer's day in Sydney, in the bar jutting out over the rocky outcrop overlooking the sparkling harbour, watching our darling Aubrey marry her man Sean, well, it might well have been one of the best of my life.

And that's saying something. I am a zillionaire after all.

Yes, I have stepped back from running Ascot Industries, leaving my very able second in charge, the right woman to take the business fully into the next century. But I am still loaded. I could buy this famous little restaurant right now if I pleased.

Except, for the first time in my life, I have no urge to conquer.

"Vivian." I turn at the sound of the deep voice calling my name.

"Enzo, my dear, I was hoping you were near. Would you mind nabbing me a drink?"

Enzo takes me by the hand, turns it over and kisses my wrist, right upon my pulse. Such a charmer.

A wallflower now, content to watch the world rather than run it, I spy Jessica and Jamie, snuggled close together on the dance floor, her hand clutched in his, his lips resting on her knuckles.

I wonder if they know she is pregnant. It's so clear to me, my gift twanging like a bell.

There's Daisy, up on stage with her man Jay. The two of them sharing a microphone, his hand wrapped around hers. Their eyes on only each other.

Just quietly, the music isn't to my taste. A little too rock and roll, when I've always had a little thing for Barry Manilow. But the crowd don't share my sentiment. The joy in the room is palpable. No wonder they've done so well for themselves.

"Ladies and gents," calls Jay, and the crowd cheers so loud my new hearing aid buzzes. "The bride and groom!"

Aubrey—dear girl—bursts through the doors in her whisper of a dress; arms spread out, fingers beckoning the cheers to continue. Such a riot, that girl. If she'd come sliding in on her knees I'd not have been surprised.

Then through the doorway, cool as you please, comes her man. All brooding bone structure and broad shoulders, that one.

Aubrey turns to him with a smile. No, a grin. Then laughter lights her face up till she's pure sunshine. While he looks at her as if she is the moon and stars, all wrapped up in one pocket-sized package.

A woman who must be Sean's mother—same dark hair and intense blue eyes—comes in behind them, Aubrey and Sean's darling little girl in her arms. A button of a child with her mother's auburn curls and father's bright blue eyes. She'll be trouble when she grows up, no doubt. But the good kind. The kind that fosters *joie de vivre*.

The little one holds out a hand and Aubrey takes her to her hip, leaving the hand for her daddy to hold. And together they move to the dance floor. A threesome, swaying and laughing and hugging, while Daisy and Jay croon a song that puts a tear even in my tough old eye.

This, all this, is more than I ever could have hoped when I gave each of my girls the nudge to go after what they needed most—the opportunity to put their fears behind them and come into their own.

The crowd parts in that moment, and there he is. My Enzo. Drink in hand.

"Bless you, dear man," I say as I take a sip of the most excellent champagne I've had shipped over for the occasion. Apparently, the groom's family are old money, but one must never leave such things to chance!

Enzo draws me close. The look in his eye makes me feel twenty-one again. The world at my feet.

"Dance with me," he croons.

"I shall," I promise. "Till I can dance no more." And so the night goes on. A night of laughter and song and love and hope and friendship and family. Of more happily-ever-afters than even I could have imagined.

It seems fairy tales do come true.

* * * * *

If you missed the previous stories in
A Fairytale Summer! trilogy,
look out for

Cinderella's New York Fling
by Cara Colter
Italian Escape with Her Fake Fiancé
by Sophie Pembroke

If you enjoyed this story,
check out these other great reads from
Ally Blake

Brooding Rebel to Baby Daddy
Crazy About Her Impossible Boss
A Week with the Best Man

All available now!